Divided Heart

by

K. M. Daughters

Divided Heart

Cover Art by *Lisa Dawn MacDonald*

The Wild Rose Press, Inc.
PO Box 708
Adams Basin, NY 14410-0708
Visit us at www.thewildrosepress.com

Publishing History
First Edition, 2025
Trade Paperback ISBN 978-1-5092-6213-7
Digital ISBN 978-1-5092-6222-9

Published in the United States of America

Dedication

For Daddy.
Thank you for writing our treasured children's books.
Especially A Kitten Called Frances

Acknowledgments

Our parents, Kay and Mickey, the K and M in K.M. Daughters, raised us to be grateful for all of life's abundant blessings. As we continue our journey creating books together our gratitude grows. For each other and the exhilaration of reaching Happily Ever Afters together. For the amazing professionals at The Wild Rose Press who continue to bring our stories to bookshelves. And for all the kind comments and reviews from our beloved readers.

Thank you to Ally Robertson our loving, lovely, kind and diplomatic, razor-sharp Editor. You are so much more than a champion of our work. You are a treasured friend. Speaking of treasured friends, thank you to Joelle Walker, our Fairy God-Editor and sister of the heart, and Nicola Martinez and Kay Lamb, our Christian books Editors and sisters in Christ.

Our deepest and personal gratitude to the angels at Northwestern Medicine and Eisenhower Healthcare for helping us navigate one of our most challenging journeys.

Thank you to our darling children and grandchildren for your love and encouragement and the tremendous fun we have together. Thank you to Tom and Nick for our personal happily-ever-afters.

And most of all, thank YOU for choosing to read K.M. Daughters.

Chapter 1

The soft brush on the back of her hand brought Cassidy out of the dream where she and Sawyer walked the streets of Chicago holding hands and laughing. In her dreams, Sawyer wasn't dead. Neither was Mom.

"Hi, Charlie." She turned on her side in bed to pet her Basset hound's soft head.

Cass ignored the drool cooling on the back of her hand from his nuzzles and smiled into his doleful eyes. Why did she choose a perpetually sad looking dog when she had moved to Redbird after her mother's death? Wasn't dog ownership supposed to elevate her spirits?

Despite Charlie's droopy demeanor, his sweet devotion to his mistress and his ecstatic tail wagging at the slightest scrap of attention helped drag Cass out of the bog of grief every morning. Plus, he was a clever little scamp, making it easy for her to train him and entertaining her no end.

She yawned widely and then gave the AI command. "What's the weather?"

"Currently it's sixty degrees and sunny. Sunny for the rest of the day with a high of seventy-five and a low of fifty-nine."

"Okay. Sounds good," she said in reaction to the electronic forecast. "Ready for your walk, Charlie?"

The dog bolted through her open bedroom door with impressive speed considering his stubby legs and low-lying belly. With a lot less oomph than her energetic pup, Cassidy followed behind him clad in her pajamas, a fleece-lined hoody, and sneaker socks.

Downstairs, she grabbed Charlie's leash off a wall hook by the back door and stooped to fasten it to his harness while he sat obediently, knowing the drill. She slipped into her running shoes, opened the door ahead of the dog and let him bound out onto the deck and trundle down the wooden stairs untethered, trailing his leash. Cassidy caught up with him where he sat on a patch of lawn at the bottom of the stairs as she had trained him. Scooping the leash up off the ground, she set out on their morning walk across her back lawn onto the wood chip lined trail that circled Redbird Lake.

Charlie snuffled and ambled making frequent stops to do his business and sniff the trunks of trees lining the path. Cassidy used the daily pre-dawn routine as a positivity meditation. Or at least, she tried to achieve daily positivity there since Mom had died six months ago. Inheriting her childhood home and deciding to sell her Chicago condo and move to Redbird returned her to the comfort of the familiar——her first and only home before adulthood.

Cassidy had always loved Redbird with its close-knit, small-town community, stunning natural beauty, and legions of cardinals roosting in the loblolly pines that ringed Redbird Lake. She cherished the memories of growing up there. Cass was the popular blonde beauty all through school who earned a full ride to Northwestern University and was the daughter of one of Redbird's favorite couples. Her dad was the town paint contractor who died of cancer when she was nineteen years old. Her mom was the owner of the local and only bookstore in

Redbird, Cozy Nook Books.

But Mom wasn't there to comfort her in the familiar and continue living their "us against the world" philosophy during all the years as a single mom. And Sawyer had died a year before Mom. No matter where Cassidy lived or worked, she was an orphan and a widow at age twenty-eight. She had yet to pull out of the mire of sadness and loneliness of loss.

She reached the turning point about a quarter of the way around the lake. "Time to go home, Charlie." She gently tugged the leash to reverse his direction.

Slipping her phone out of the pocket of her hoody, she took a couple of sunrise photos of the lake mirroring the pastel lavender, rose, and peach streaked sky. The late June weather was mild and perfect for walking or hiking—her favorite pastimes. Cass inhaled the pine scented air. Her gaze lingered on a fire engine red cardinal flitting in the branches of a towering tree. She captured a photo of him mid-flight despite the bounty of cardinal images in her photo library already.

Reaching the steps off her deck, Cass dropped Charlie's leash. He thumped up the stairs and sat in front of the door while she opened the door of a storage area and filled three bird feeders with seeds. After hanging the feeders in trees on the perimeter of her yard, she mounted the steps and ushered Charlie inside.

The roasted nut aroma of brewed coffee from her programmed pot greeted her in the sunny kitchen. The walls were painted pale lemon. Early morning sunshine poured through the lake-facing window over the sink. Even when the weather was cloudy or stormy, somehow Mom's kitchen décor brightened the day.

She poured a mug full of coffee, added a splash of

milk, filled Charlie's food and water bowls, set them down on the floor and then settled on a bar stool at her kitchen counter in front of her laptop. Scanning her email messages drove home her daily reality: no one wrote to her, and she wrote to no one.

The rumble of a motor and a car door slam took her away from her robotic junk mail deleting and drew her to the front of the house. The white van stenciled with Corrigan's Paint Contracting insignia was parked on her gravel driveway. Rina bounded toward her front door carrying a bakery box.

Cassidy preempted her best friend's doorbell ring and swung open the front door.

"Yay, you're up." Rina breezed in front of Cass and marched toward the kitchen without breaking stride.

"Good morning to you, too, Katherine," Cass muttered.

She closed the door and trailed Rina who had always treated Cassidy's home as if it were her own. Rina ferreted inside kitchen cabinets for plates and a coffee mug and then slid open the utensils' drawer.

"What did you bring us?" Cass pulled up a stool. She propped a crooked elbow on the countertop and cradled her chin in her cupped hand watching Rina "fix" breakfast.

"Varrelman's crumb coffee cake fresh from the oven. Your fav." Rina untied the string on the box and slid a knife out of the butcher block holder on the counter. Waving the knife in the air, she said, "I picked it up when they opened this morning."

"Oh yum. A big slice, please."

"Well, duh." Rina wielded the knife and brought two plates over to the counter in front of Cass. She set the plates down, rounded the corner of the bar and sat on the stool next to Cassidy.

"How come you're driving Mickey's truck? Doesn't he have work?" Cass said.

"Yes, he does, so I can only stay a few minutes. The truck was blocking my car in the driveway, so I nabbed it for my breakfast delivery. Mickey gave his blessing. Oh, and sends his love."

"Back to him. How's business going?" Cass said, her mouth full of buttery deliciousness.

"Good. Picking up now that the weather is nice. Your dad would be proud."

"He was always proud of Mickey even as a high school kid apprenticing with him during the summers. That's why he handed over the keys to his shop to Mickey when he learned he was sick."

"I know. You have no idea what that meant to my husband. He was practically a kid himself when your dad died. Only twenty-one and still searching for a career. And he was able to walk into a well-run business doing something he was good at. Thanks to your dad's mentoring him. He treated him like a son."

"Well Daddy always wanted a boy. To carry on the Corrigan name."

"Oh bull. Your father wouldn't have traded you for the world. Besides, Mickey *is* carrying on the Corrigan name with the business."

Rina licked her index finger, swept it over her plate to vacuum crumbs and then popped it in her mouth. "Yum. That was so worth the calories."

She hopped off her stool. "Done with your plate, Cass?"

Cassidy held out her empty dish. "I am. That was so

good. Thank you."

"You're welcome." Rina's gaze locked on Cassidy's left hand. "Oh my gosh, you took off your wedding ring!"

Instinctively Cassidy balled her hand into a fist and rested it in her lap out of view. "I…"

"I'm so proud of you. That's a big step." Rina circled her arms around Cass's shoulders and gave her a squeeze. "So now maybe I can set something up with you and Mickey's brother?"

Cassidy's stomach clenched and anxiety shimmered through her at the thought of dating another man besides Sawyer. "No, no, Rina. Not yet. I just…"

She closed her eyes for a moment to blot out the worried expression on Rina's pretty face. Then she plastered a smile on her face and regarded her lifelong friend. "It's a baby step for me, sweetie. I just…I guess I just felt like it was time. I think I've grown stronger and more at peace with Sawyer's death since I started working at the store."

Inheriting and running the bookstore the past months was Cassidy's saving grace. Cozy Nook Books was the only place where her deep-seated grief abated fully. She remembered her mom's sweet presence there. Even more powerfully, it seemed that Sawyer was there with her every day like a heavenly hug. She had met him at Cozy Nook during an author book signing.

The gorgeous coffee table book of his breathtaking photographs throughout his celebrated career was a huge magnet for the community and a very lucrative signing event for Cassidy's mother. Meeting Sawyer that day had Cass believing in love at first sight. With Sawyer, she was justified in that belief up until the day he died a year and a half ago.

"All right, Cass. I promise I'll be patient." Rina turned towards the sink, dishes in hand.

Patient? My firecracker Rina? No way. "Thanks. I promise I'll keep trying."

Rina yanked on the stainless-steel handle of the dishwasher and opened the door. Stooping to stack in the dishes, she held out her hand. "Can I have your fork, please?"

Cassidy got off her stool and put the fork in the utensils' basket in the washer herself. "Still dropping by the Nook later to help with the author signing this afternoon?"

"Of course. Wouldn't miss it. What time should I be there?"

"I'm leaving as soon as I shower and dress. So, any time before the one o'clock story hour is good. It's such a cute book. I think the kids will love it."

"I know I'll love being there for a children's book signing." Rina dried her hands on a dish towel a shadow of sadness glimmering in her eyes.

Katherine aka Rina Lynch and Cassidy Corrigan had always adored kids. When they were small, they played "little mommies" bundling baby dolls into strollers, changing their water-wet diapers, feeding them with magic milk and juice disappearing bottles, and rocking blanket-wrapped dolls to "sleep."

Cass had married Sawyer months after college graduation. They had planned on seeing the world for five years or so before starting a family. They'd only been married less than three years when Sawyer was diagnosed with ALS.

Rina had married Mickey shortly after she graduated

college the same year as Cass. But she would have broken out the champagne had she conceived on her wedding night. Six years later she had suffered three miscarriages. It was a touchy subject that Cass never broached knowing that Rina would confide details in her when she was ready. Cass thought that Rina and Mickey were still hopeful and trying to conceive.

Cass prayed regularly that her treasured friend could have the boisterous, firecracker family of her dreams.

"So, kiddo, I'm out of here." Rina pecked a kiss on Cassidy's cheek. "See ya in an hour or two."

"Bye, honey."

Charlie snoozed on his fluffy cushion in a patch of sunlight streaming through the sliding glass doors between her breakfast nook and the deck. Cass admired the panorama of the pine tree-rimmed, sun dappled lake and then headed upstairs to get ready for the event at the store.

Fresh from a shower, she stood in her walk-in closet with a towel tucked around her deciding on what to wear. She chose a cornflower blue, silk midi dress. She might not wear Sawyer's ring anymore. But she could wear his favorite dress.

Chapter 2

The sun crested the pine trees encircling the lake casting their deep green reflections on the water's surface. Ty Martin swept the brush across the canvas capturing the changing light that filtered through the floor to ceiling glass windows in his studio creating patterns of yellow, red and lavender shimmers on the pure white walls.

Music blared from speakers hung from the ceiling. Ty tapped his foot in time with the heavy beat as he added the sun's exploding colors across the lake to his painting and then stood back assessing his work with a critical eye.

Satisfied with his progress so far, he rubbed his back and turned away from his easel. Ty paced toward the red mini fridge in the corner of the room, passing by canvases propped against the walls. He opened the refrigerator door, grabbed a protein drink, unscrewed the top and chugged half of it before stopping to take a breath.

He returned to the easel and spent the next couple of hours adding tiny touches that made the lake come to life with almost photographic realism. His eyes blurred as he checked the clock on top of the fridge.

Seven o'clock? No wonder my stomach is growling.

Ty had painted through the night, missing meals and sleep to complete the piece on his easel, one of many included in his upcoming gallery show in Chicago. He needed a shower and ten hours uninterrupted rest. He wiped his hands on a damp towel hanging off the easel, chugged the rest of the shake and took a moment to gaze out the window drinking in the beautiful vista.

Buying his house and renovating it had taken a full year, but it was worth every minute and every dollar that it took to make his home move-in ready. The architect and building contractor had followed his specifications for his art studio precisely. He had left the rest of the house's interior design to his mom and sister. Ty finally had a place he could call home.

Stretching his arms up over his head, he yawned widely and then ambled downstairs to the second floor into his spacious bedroom suite. Ty stripped and tossed his clothes into a heap on the bathroom tile floor next to a double-sized, walk-in shower. The muscles in his back started to relax under the pounding spray. He increased the water temperature until his skin reddened and steam filled the shower.

Turning off the nozzle, he dried off with a towel. Naked and only slightly invigorated, Ty dragged himself into his bedroom and fell face down on his king-sized bed. As exhaustion started to overtake him the landline phone on his bedside table rang. Since only his family had that number, he answered the call on the third ring.

"Yeah?" he growled.

"Pleasant and cheerful as usual, little brother," came Kane's sibling sarcasm.

"I just got to sleep, old man, so this better be good."

His identical twin chuckled at Ty's old man description of him. They had a running joke about age. Kane was five minutes older than Ty.

"Just got to sleep? Were you out partying all night again?" Kane teased.

"I wish. I got immersed in creating a painting and I lost track of time. And meals. You know all about that."

"Yep. Been there, done that with a musical score. Sorry to drop this on you but I have to ask a favor."

"No problem. What do you need?" Ty shifted to sit on the edge of the bed, sleep forgotten. Family always came first.

"Maggie threw up all night long and hasn't stopped yet this morning. She has morning sickness round the clock. This little one is giving Mommy a hard time to say the least. She's supposed to be there in Redbird for the book signing this afternoon."

Ty rubbed his eyes. "Right. I didn't realize that's today. Lost track of the date, too."

"There's no way she can rally," Kane continued. "It's too late to cancel and reschedule and she doesn't want to let the little ones down. She was supposed to read the book at the bookstore's story hour. And then autograph any books the kids' parents buy. I know this is a lot to ask if you've been working all night, but could you possibly go and do the book signing and reading in her place?"

"Me? Will the store be okay with that? Maggie wrote the book, not me."

"Maggie believes that you're just as much a part of the book as she is. You brought Frances to life with your illustrations and your name is on the front cover, too. She thinks the owner of the bookstore will be fine with the substitution."

"What time do I have to be there?"

"You'll do it?"

"Of course I'll do it. You know I'd do anything for Mags." He entered his closet, slipped a yellow polo shirt off a hanger, shrugged the portable phone against his ear and pulled the shirt over his head.

"We owe you big time. The event starts at one o'clock, but Maggie said you should get there early to help set up. It's at the Cozy Nook Books store on Park Avenue."

"I've passed that shop a couple of times and have been meaning to stop in and check it out."

"Thanks, Ty. I really appreciate this."

"Tell Mags I hope she feels better. Take good care of her."

Ty pulled on a pair of black jeans and strode into the bathroom to shave. In the mirror, his ebony hair curled against his collar. He raked his fingers through the damp unruly curls and then grabbed his cell phone off the charger to set a reminder to schedule a haircut before his showing.

He had time to spare before he had to leave the house, so he returned to his studio to organize the paintings to send to the gallery in downtown Chicago. He debated sending the large painting of the little blue-eyed kitten, deciding against it. Frances the kitten belonged to his niece, and he would give Harper the painting the next time that she visited him.

Done with sorting gallery art, he wandered over to his desk to check emails on his laptop computer. When Ty finally joined the world again after days passing in a blur while painting, he marveled at the number of messages that stuffed his Inbox. Scanning the list, he deleted all but three.

Ty read the message marked with an "urgent" red

exclamation point from his ex-girlfriend, Melanie. In all caps, she demanded that he answer her texts which he had purposefully ignored for weeks. Things had not gone well with that relationship. He had made his first mistake when he had given in to her relentless badgering and had agreed to let her move in to the condo that he rented from his brother. Ty had known from the start that she wasn't the one.

His second mistake was not having realized that Melanie didn't get him. He certainly didn't get her. They had lived together for a few mostly miserable months while she had bombarded him with complaints about everything, especially his abandonment of her to his art. He hadn't known how to fix things and pretty much hadn't cared if they worked things out, opting to continue to lose himself in his work. Melanie had moved out and had moved on without so much as leaving a note which had ultimately come as a relief to Ty.

Is she trying to come back into my life now? He deleted the email.

Before he left the house, Ty walked through his spacious living room, slid the glass door open and drifted out onto the deck overlooking the lake. The view of Redbird Lake alone had sold him on the house. He closed his eyes and took deep breaths of the pine-scented air. Opening his eyes to soak up more of his favorite view, he caught sight of a candy apple red cardinal perched on the deck railing five feet away from him, seemingly staring directly at Ty's face. He itched to paint the brilliant-colored male and took a mental snapshot so that he could bring the bird to life on canvas as soon as he could get back to work.

He tore his gaze away from the natural beauty,

ducked back into the house, grabbed his keys and wallet off the kitchen counter and bounded out the door. Outside he encountered the mailman coming up the path to the front door with a package in hand. Ty accepted the delivery, checked the return address, and smiled.

His mother, the proud of owner of the famous company, Kamille's Kookies, had sent him a box of cookies once a month like clockwork since his first year away at college. When Ty had told her that he had more than outgrown the need for care packages, she had persisted anyway.

"You will always be my little boy, and I worry you don't eat enough," she stubbornly maintained.

Ty long since didn't have roommates to help him gobble up the goodies, but the monthly boxes kept coming. From the weight of that shipment, Mom had sent *more* than a month's supply. Perfect timing, he thought. The kids at the story hour would love the cookies and supplying treats might help eliminate any disappointment over his representing the book instead of Maggie.

He pressed the ignition button, and his truck engine roared to life. Toby Keith's voice blared through the multi-speaker sound system filling the cabin with heart pumping music. Donning aviator sunglasses, he backed out of the driveway and proceeded towards Main Street in downtown Redbird.

Ty couldn't believe his luck when he found a parking spot in front of Coffee & More after only driving around the block twice—a new record for him. He tossed his sunglasses on the passenger seat and hopped out of the truck. A couple of old men slowly trundled towards the coffee shop. Ty hurried ahead of them to hold the door open for them.

"Thank you, young man," one of the men bellowed. Ty took note of the discreet hearing aids in the man's ears. "You are a gentleman."

Ty smiled in response waiting for them to shuffle inside the shop in front of him. He was about to enter behind the two men when a vision in blue, waiting to exit on the other side of the door, stopped him in his tracks. Describing the woman holding an extra-large go-cup as beautiful was pure understatement.

He beckoned her through the open door with a wave of his hand. "After you."

"Thank you so much." She tugged at the briefcase strap over her shoulder and walked toward him.

Hardly as tall as his shoulder, she swept past Ty trailing the scent of honeysuckles.

"Yes, you are a gentleman," she said softly.

She never looked back, but Ty could not tear his gaze away from her retreating figure, her *very attractive* retreating figure. She turned at the next corner and disappeared out of sight. He continued to stare at the empty sidewalk. Something about the gorgeous stranger seemed momentous as if he had a glimpse of his destiny. Shaking his head, he chalked his reaction up to a lack of sleep and strode into the shop to order much needed coffee.

"Hey, Ty." The owner greeted him as he took a seat at the counter. "The usual?"

"Not today, Mirela. I'm in a bit of a hurry and I don't have time to eat, but I'll take a double coffee to go."

"No time to eat? Pshh." She placed a warm blueberry muffin in front of him and poured a steaming cup of black coffee. "There's always time to eat."

"Why does everyone try to feed me? Do I look undernourished?" he grumbled.

The shop waitress zipped by him toting a tray of dirty dishes. "Oh honey," she said. "You look mighty fine to me. I wouldn't change a thing." She winked at him and cackled.

"Thanks, Jeannie." He grinned at her, used to her overt flirting. She was old enough to be his mother.

Ty took a big bite of the delicious warm muffin oozing blueberries and was glad that he did.

"Why the hurry today?" Mirela brought a large carry-out container of coffee over to the counter.

"I'm filling in for my sister-in-law at the bookstore. She was supposed to sign the children's book she wrote today, but she's having horrible morning sickness. So instead of cancelling she asked if I would cover for her."

"That sounds exciting. I didn't know they were having a kids' event at the Nook. I'll call my daughter to tell her to bring my granddaughter. What time does it start?"

Ty checked his watch. "In a couple of hours. I better get going. I want to help the owner set up." He stood and put money on the counter and grabbed the coffee. "Thank you for the muffin. It hit the spot."

He drove the truck into the small parking lot on Park Avenue adjacent to the bookstore. Carrying the coffee and the box of cookies, he stopped outside Cozy Nook Books to admire the huge poster displayed in the window announcing the book signing that day.

A flash of blue through the plate glass caught his eye. The woman from the coffee shop stood behind the counter in the bookstore triggering him to grin from ear to ear.

This day just got a whole lot better. He reached for the door handle.

Chapter 3

Cassidy noticed the man from the coffee shop tugging one-handed on the locked door handle of her bookstore. But it took a few minutes for her to move away from the counter and pace toward the door. She remained in a daze from what seemed like a fleeting glimpse of the hereafter earlier.

Off balance. Off kilter. That morning kept getting stranger making her head spin. The extremely hot man who stood outside her shop holding a gigantic bakery box in his arms had sparked dizzying attraction in her earlier on her coffee run—something she had thought impossible since Sawyer had died.

As she had unlocked the employee entrance of her shop, she had lingered dreamily in the memory of the man's handsome face, his impressive physique, and mesmerizing gray-blue eyes. Cass wasn't so far out of the romance game to miss genuine interest from the opposite sex—and, although subtle, the man *had* displayed interest.

Steeped in her happy reverie, Cassie had zipped through the motions of readying the store for customers: switching on lights, powering up her retail database, checking her cash drawer and double checking her inventory for the signing. She had moved through the familiar routine humming softly... and apparently grinning.

Because Sawyer's voice came from behind her, "Sunshine smile."

She had frozen in place at the familiar phrase as if jerked to halt like a cartoon character hooked around the neck. Her husband had always professed to love her smile describing it as pure sunshine. Cass had longed to hear his distinctive booming voice again…see his face…kiss his lips. But?

Cassidy had hung in her tracks for seconds weighing whether or not to turn around. If confronted with a vision of Sawyer, would she feel more or less grief addled? Was it better to imagine hearing a voice rather than to search for a spectral speaker?

Sucking in a breath, Cass had slowly pivoted and then she had clapped a hand over her mouth blinking her eyes repeatedly trying to dispel disbelief. Sawyer sat at the table in the alcove of the shop where every book signing had historically taken place, including Sawyer's on the day when she had first met him.

She had wanted to race into his arms to grab ahold of the man and never let go. But her limbs hadn't cooperated, and her chance had evaporated. Sawyer's loving face had shimmered and disappeared leaving her shaken and incredulous and questioning her sanity.

Sinking down into the chair that Sawyer had just occupied in her imagination, she had relived cherished memories in that exact spot in the shop. She had earned her college degree and had decided to take the summer to spend time with her mother in Redbird, help out at the bookstore during the high season and deal with sorting out her future career in the fall. That summer, Cass had met Sawyer.

The morning was sunny and sweltering. An air

conditioner repair man clanked around in the shop's utility room attempting to resurrect the cooling system – they hoped at least long enough to pull off the well-publicized book signing that afternoon. The expected turnout was epic for the town. Sawyer Finnegan, the award-winning, Chicago native, photojournalist had agreed to appear at only one book signing to launch his rumored breathtaking coffee table book—Cozy Nook Books in Redbird, Illinois.

Neither Mom nor Cassidy had a clue why he had chosen to honor their little shop, but they were determined to make sure that Sawyer didn't regret his singular decision.

Despite his iconic status in the contemporary world of celebrity and world leaders' photo-portraiture, Sawyer's unassuming reputation preceded him. True to form, he arrived at the shop five minutes before the appointed event time wearing crisp jeans, a white V-neck, short-sleeve, cotton T-shirt, and thick-soled work boots. Just a regular guy who commanded thousands of dollars for a session in front of his lens.

He was classically handsome Black Irish with a chiseled jaw line, fair skin, low fade cut raven hair, a tall, slim physique, Celtic features and dancing, powder blue eyes. When he trained his eyes on Cass, she felt caught up in a tractor beam.

She welcomed him, somehow overcoming awkwardness in the thrall of instant attraction, seated him in the alcove and provided him with the requested sharpie and bottled water. Then she had helped her mom with customer relations. Manning the register in the thankfully cool shop, her attention riveted on the charming man of the hour. Cass couldn't tear her gaze away from Sawyer and he, apparently, was just as smitten. In between chatting up autograph hounds, his eyes sought her out and locked on her with increasing intensity.

By the end of the event, Cassidy and Sawyer had already fallen in love with each other. He lingered behind the last customer offering to help close the store. Her mother poo-pooed having helpmates, maybe sensing the sparks between them. Mom instead suggested that Cass buy Sawyer a drink to toast his successful book launch or possibly treat him to dinner.

Sawyer immediately accepted the invitation to the town's only bar and grill. A bottle of wine, a steak dinner and slow dancing to juke box music later, Cass and Sawyer knew that they had found their soulmates.

The mystery of Sawyer's having chosen Cozy Nook Books for his launch was solved. His family had spent summers renting cottages near Redbird Lake when he was a kid. That summer he had rented a lakefront house there. Cass spent more time at his rental than in her own home.

They were engaged on the 4th of July because he thought only fireworks would do for the occasion. They married in early September in the enchanting Chapel on the Lake, a fairy tale dream come true for Cass. And then they had lived the most romantic happily ever after.

Cass had closed her eyes homing in on Sawyer's spectral appearance where she had sat. Was the chair warmer or colder beneath her? No. Did she detect his boundless energy, his electric touch? No, neither. But a sense of his presence had remained. And although rattled, that had given her welcome peace.

She disengaged the bolt lock, motioned to the man to take a step back, opened the door, stepped through the threshold, and propped it open leaning her back against the glass.

"Looks like it's my turn to be chivalrous this morning and hold the door for you," she said with a smile. "But we're not open yet, sir."

"I know I'm here early," Ty said. "For the book signing. I tried to call first, but there was no answer."

He's here for a children's book signing? Where's his child?

"I just got here about a half hour ago…well, you know since we met at the coffee shop…Anyway…" Cass trailed off.

"I do remember seeing you at the coffee shop."

He held out his hand. "And it's Ty. Ty Martin, not sir."

Cass gave his hand a light shake, ruffled by the instant swelling of attraction at his simple touch. "Um…hello. I'm Cassidy Finnegan. This is my store."

"Great to meet you officially, Cassidy. Let me put these cookies somewhere and I can give you a hand setting up."

He breezed past her leaving in his wake the scents of citrus-musk aftershave and sweet wafts of chocolate from that bakery box.

She stalked behind him. "Why are you offering to help me, Ty? Honestly, I'm confused about why you're here at all."

Ty set the box down on the counter and turned to face her. "Didn't my brother or sister-in-law call you? I thought Kane took care of that."

"Kane? I'm sorry, I don't know these people. Do I?"

He tilted his head and huffed a laugh. "Honestly, I don't know if you've met Maggie or not. But I'm here for her."

Cass knit her brow. "Maggie, as in Maggie Martin, the author?"

"Yep. *A Kitten Called Frances.* Mags is my sister-in-law. And she's currently hugging the white bowl. Vicious morning sickness."

Her stomach fell digesting the implications. "Oh no," she groaned. "I'm so sorry to hear that. But what the heck am I going to do with all the kids?"

"No worries, if you'll have me. Kane—that's my brother and Maggie's husband—asked me to substitute at the event. I'll take her place."

Her thoughts scrambled shifting gears. "I advertised a supervised story hour so that parents can drop off the kids and have some time to themselves. And then an author signing. Maggie hasn't pre-signed any copies…"

"Again, no worries. I'll read to the kids. And sign books later for your customers."

"But…I'm not sure that's…"

Ty touched her arm, a soft brush that carried a sensuous slam to her senses. "Do you have a copy of the book?"

"Of course. Why?"

"Humor me."

"I haven't unpacked the books yet," she said. "Come with me. I'd love a hand setting out the inventory as long as you're here to help."

In the back room, Cass pointed out the shipping cartons. Ty picked up a copy and pointed to the bylines. "See here? Illustrated by T. Binder. That's me."

"Oh my gosh. I *love* your drawings. This is one of

the most beautifully illustrated books I've ever seen," she gushed. "And I've seen a *lot* of children's books."

He beamed at her hoisting up the shipping carton in one smooth, effortless motion. "Thanks. It was fun working with my sister-in-law. I actually found Frances, the infamous kitten, right here in Redbird."

"Really? So, it isn't pure fiction?"

"Some," he said. "But the bones are true. Where do want these?"

"Well, since you're the author for today, I'll let you decide how you want the books available at the signing table. Follow me."

Cass led him to the alcove grateful that revisiting the spot where she thought she had seen her dead husband brought no other worldly vibes. "This is where you'll sit for the signing. As for the story hour, wherever you think you'll be comfortable."

"Hm." He surveyed the alcove area. "I think I'll stack the books on and behind the table for later."

He pointed to an open, carpeted section in front of the shelves in the children's book area of the store. "Maybe right there for the reading?"

"Perfect. We can make that work. I'll stack these books," she said.

"I'll go get the other carton."

Watching him walk away with easy athletic grace was a treat. The man had seriously great buns. She had noticed the cut of his black jeans and the biceps- hugging yellow polo shirt he wore from her first glimpse of him at Coffee & More. Tall, dark and handsome. With a killer smile. And extremely talented judging from the book that she held in her hand. A *very* appealing man to Cassidy.

A rap on the door sounded and Cassidy looked toward the front of the store. Rina peered through the glass and gave a quick wave when Cass's eyes met hers.

She hustled over and opened the door. Energizer bunny Rina blew past her into the shop. "Okay. What do you want me to do first?"

"Whoa…" Rina pulled up short at the counter eyeing the bakery box. "Kamille's Kookies?" she squealed. "Where did you get these?"

Ty appeared toting a box.

"From me," he said. "Kamille is my mother."

"She's your *mother?*" Cass and Rina chorused.

Rina began working open the knotted string on the box. "You know Kamille Martin's son? Why did I not know this, Cass?"

"We just met today, Rina. Ty, this is my best friend and Kamille's Kookies lover, Katherine Lynch."

He set the box down on the floor and offered Rina a handshake. "Good to meet you, Katherine."

"Rina, please." She accepted his handshake. "Are you vacationing in Redbird, Ty?"

"No. I recently bought a house on the Lake. Moved here from Chicago."

"Welcome. Was it by any chance the Simpson property? The one with a two-story deck and the boat dock?"

"It is."

"I love that house." Rina faced Cass, her eyes glowing. "You and Ty are practically neighbors, Cass."

What a happy thought.

"I guess we are." She smiled warmly at him. "Ty is here for the event. He's the illustrator of the book."

"Oh, wow. That's great." Rina opened the bakery

box. "Can I steal one of these before I go to work?"

Ty muscled the inventory box off the floor. "Sure. I'll stack these for you, Cassidy."

Chapter 4

Ty emptied the second shipping carton and arranged the hardcover books around the designated autograph table. He half-listened to Cassie's and Rina's lively conversation liking even the sound of the bookshop owner's soft voice. He had assumed when he had volunteered to save the day for his sister-in-law that he would have to suffer through the out of his comfort zone ordeal. Discovering that the stunning woman who had captured his attention at the coffee shop was running the book signing event had changed his mind.

Plus, there was something about the charming bookshop itself that tugged at him. The place made him feel welcomed as if he belonged there. Sun beams slanted through spotless plate glass windows casting butterscotch-colored glimmers against the pale peach-colored walls. Rows of clearly marked solid wood shelving divided books into reading categories. A vintage wooden table to the left of the front door held a display of new releases. Another, surely one of a kind, vintage table displayed *New York Times* Best Sellers. The main counter, too, was made of carved wood and gave off an antique vibe.

The doors of an armoire-like piece of furniture which tucked into a corner near the front window display were ajar. An arrangement of bookmarks, reading lights, mugs, and reading accessories on the inside shelves enticed book lover customers. A pair of wing-backed chairs grouped directly opposite the armoire invited readers to sit, thumb through a novel, and make themselves comfortable.

"My drink's gone cold. How about yours, Ty?" came Cassie's sweet voice.

"Probably." He emptied the last of the shipping box.

"Okay." She bustled over to the counter and scooped up their paper cups. "I'll warm them in the microwave. Be right back."

"Are you done over there, Ty? I could use a hand setting out the chairs for the kids," Rina said.

"Sure." He followed Rina who tore into the back room like she ran a race.

She pointed out the rows of stacked kindergarten-sized, wooden chairs next to the rows of shelves where Cass housed her boxed inventory.

"I'll bring them out front to you," he said. "I want the story hour set up next to the children's bookshelves."

She nodded agreement and spun on her heel returning to the main area of the store.

Hefting four chairs at a time, two in each arm, Ty made eight back and forth trips between the back room to the front of the shop bringing tiny seats to the story hour area. Rina arranged the chairs in half circles around a central rocking chair. Ty eyed the storyteller seat of honor mentally dismissing actually sitting there when the time came to read to the kids. Being on their level was more Ty's style.

Cassidy emerged from the kitchenette off the storage area. Her peacock blue dress swished against her long, shapely legs and the curled tendrils of her long blonde hair bounced against her shoulders. She toted a hot cup in each hand. His senses filled with her soft floral scent when she drew near him and handed him his drink.

"Thanks," he said. He took a quick sip. "Anything else you want done to set up?"

"Uh huh. Can you hold this a second?" She held out her paper cup.

"Sure." He took the cup out of her hand.

Cass scurried to the back of the store. She returned cradling a helium tank in one arm. A large plastic bag of multi-colored balloons dangled from her other hand. "The kids love the balloons. I like to go a little crazy filling the shop with them."

"Crazy, it is," he said with a smile. "You and Rina relax a bit. I'll inflate these for you."

"No, no, we'll help," Cass protested. "Rina and I can tie the strings and place them around the shop."

He drifted over to the counter, set the coffee cups down and then paced back to join Cass and Rina.

"So…" He fitted a yellow balloon on the tank nozzle and let the helium flow. "Do you host story hours here often?"

"Yes. Once a month when I receive new releases inventory, for sure. If we're lucky enough to schedule an author signing for a children's book, like Maggie Martin, we work with the author availability regardless of the slated story hours."

"You want a knot?" he said when the first balloon was full.

"Please," Cass said.

Ty complied and then handed the balloon over, choosing a green one next to put the balloon-filling conveyor belt in motion. He knotted it and handed it to Rina for stringing.

"Rina mentioned we're neighbors," Ty said. "Do you live on Redbird Lake, too?"

"I do. Just about a direct line across the lake from your property." Cassidy let the yellow balloon fly to nestle against the ceiling, the string dangling.

"I'm really enjoying the view from my deck," he said. "Now the view got a whole lot better."

The porcelain skin on her cheeks blushed pinkish and she dipped her eyes regarding him through her lashes. The upward motion of her arms sending the balloon upward had focused Ty's attention on her hands. No wedding ring.

Good. Very good.

She grinned at Ty. "We'll float the balloons just out of reach of the little ones. They can take a balloon or two home with them after the event."

The trio worked in rhythm until Cass declared, "If we blow up just one more, the first customer through the door might send all these balloons down Park Avenue."

"So, we're done?" Rina said.

"Yes. Thank you for helping," Cass replied. She picked up the half full bag of balloons and helium tank.

"Good." Rina rubbed her hands together. "My fingers are cramping from tying strings. And you're welcome."

"I'll go stow this stuff in back. You guys want to join me to relax a bit before the kids arrive? We can finish our morning drinks, Ty," Cassidy proposed.

"Sure," Ty said.

"I'm going to dash to Coffee & More for a latte," Rina said. "Do you guys want anything?"

"I'm good," he said.

"Me, too," Cassidy agreed. "Lord knows we have

plenty of cookies here, thanks to Ty."

"Save me one or two." Rina opened the door gingerly, eying the swaying balloons, and then took off down Park Avenue.

Ty picked up his and Cass's cups and followed her to the back of the store. She directed him to two chairs set in front of an ornately carved, antique wooden desk. "Please, have a seat."

He sat down on the chair, crossed his left leg resting his ankle on his right knee, and leaned against the seatback, coffee cup in hand. Ty took a sip. Cassidy chose to sit across from him behind the desk. He met her green-eyed gaze and felt instantly connected and powerfully attracted to the lovely woman. He was unexpectedly happy at the twist of fate that had brought him to a book signing. Ty was lost admiring her beauty and couldn't tear his gaze away from her smiling face.

Cass broke eye contact first. "The illustrations in the book are beautiful. Is that what you do for a living?"

"No. Maggie's book is the first and only time I've drawn book illustrations. I enjoyed it, but it's not really my thing. I'm an artist by trade."

"Wow. That's fascinating. What's your medium?"

"I paint with oils, acrylics, watercolors. I do gallery shows in the city."

"I would love to see your paintings."

He beamed her a smile. "That could be arranged."

"I don't get into the city often since I moved back to Redbird. But I love Chicago. I lived there for years."

"Whereabouts?"

"I lived near the Northwestern campus in a terrible, two-bedroom apartment for four years when I was in college there. Rina and I were roommates. And then I moved to a townhouse in Lincoln Park when I was married."

A shadow darkened her jade eyes, and she bit the corner of her lip.

No ring on her finger and she used the past tense. *Divorced? Should I ask?*

She spared his prying by volunteering, "My husband passed away a while ago."

"I'm very sorry for your loss," he said.

"Thank you."

There was no missing the pained expression on her face.

"Why Redbird? And why a shopkeeper? Did you have a retail business in Chicago?"

"No. I majored in library sciences. After graduating college, I worked in the Chicago Public Library system. Books are in my blood, I guess you could say. Cozy Nook Books was founded by my mom. I practically lived here when I was a kid and as soon as I turned sixteen, I worked here part-time during the school year and full-time every summer. My mother passed away recently, and I inherited the shop and the house on the Lake where I grew up. My dad passed away many years ago and I'm an only child."

"Now I'm doubly sorry for your loss," he said. No wonder shadows swam in her eyes relating to what had to be devastating sources of grief. "Are you okay, Cass?"

She huffed a sigh and cast her eyes toward the ceiling before meeting his gaze. "I'm getting there. I love it here in Redbird and I do love running the shop. My mom built its reputation over the years. We attract big name authors, like Maggie Martin, and have a very devoted clientele extending to all parts of Illinois. I'm very fortunate that the folks around here strongly support small business."

Ty chuckled. "Maggie would be *very* thrilled to hear you describe her as a big name. This is her first book."

"And already on the best seller lists," she said.

"Yeah. I'm really proud of her. My brother is beyond proud."

"Your brother must be very proud of you, too. Gallery artist and all that."

"It's mutual. He's pretty celebrated himself. Ever hear of H. Binder Martin?"

"Holy cow, yes. He's your brother?"

"Yep."

"And your mom is Kamille? What a powerhouse family."

Ty grinned at her. "They are a *lot.* I have three brothers and a sister. Two nieces and a niece or nephew on the way—hence Maggie's morning sickness. My immediate family's get togethers are chaotic fun. Add in a large extended family and…watch out."

Her sweet smile warmed his heart. He hoped his small talk helped temporarily banish her grief. Ty hardly knew her but already he wanted to give her reasons to smile.

"It must be wonderful to have a big family," she said. "I think I would like chaotic fun."

He resolved to include her the next time his family came to visit—if she would accept his invitation.

A bell jingled.

"The front door of the shop just opened," she said.

Cass was half out of her seat when Rina appeared in the back room's doorway.

"You should have seen the long line at the coffee

shop," Rina groused.

She barged into the room, flounced into the chair next to him and then took a sip from her cup. "Yum. Worth the wait, though. What did I miss?"

"Not much," Ty said.

"Ty is a gallery artist," Cass said.

"No kidding? Galleries in Chicago? Do I know your work?" Rina said.

"Yes, I show in Chicago galleries. In addition to quite a few national showings."

"What did you say your last name was again, Ty?"

"My last name is Martin."

"Nope. Doesn't ring a bell. I haunted a lot of art galleries when I lived in the city."

"I sign my canvases T. Binder. It's a family name."

Rina's eyes widened and she stared at him open-mouthed. "Did you hear that, Cassie?"

"I did…"

The bell on the front door of the shop sounded again.

"Oops," Cass said. "We can't wait to talk with you more about your work, Ty. But for now, I think you are the author for the day. The kiddos are arriving."

"My debut is about to begin." Ty chuckled. "Let's go sell some books."

Chapter 5

Cassidy watched the drop-off parade for the story hour with increasing amusement at the emerging pattern of behavior. A frazzled mother ushered a child through the door and invariably stood in her tracks gaping at Ty who towered over the circle of tiny wooden chairs in gorgeous splendor beaming at the customers. She couldn't take her eyes off the man, either.

Before steering their kids over to him, the women dug sunglasses out of purses to cover make-up free eyes and ran fingers through windblown hair.

Welcoming his little charges, he crouched down to each child's level, asked his or her name, and spent a few minutes talking. The way he focused his attention and the delight shining in the little ones' eyes touched Cassidy's heart.

Joelle stood next to her and covered her heart with her hand. "Oh my," she whispered. "What a stud. Who *is* he?"

Cassidy, Rina and Joelle were inseparable since high school, there for each other through the most difficult times with love and laughter.

"Maggie Larsen, the author of the featured story hour book, couldn't be here today. Ty is filling in for her, thank goodness. I would have hated to cancel the event." Cass didn't take her eyes off Ty. He laughed at something a little boy named Mark said and his appeal to her multiplied.

"Where have you been hiding him?" Joelle nudged Cassidy playfully.

"I just met him this morning. He's the illustrator of the book."

The last of the children straggled in and took the remaining seats. The mothers who usually dropped the kids off and ran back out the door to do errands or rushed away to have a little time to themselves seemed reluctant to leave at all. Outside, they still gawked at Ty through the glass as they walked past the shop.

Cassidy paced over and joined Ty standing in front of the children. "Good morning, everyone," she said.

"Good morning, Miss Cassidy," came a high-pitched chorus of voices.

"We have an extra special treat today. Mister Ty Martin is here to read a book to you this morning. And guess what?"

The kids played along. "What?"

"Mr. Martin drew *all* the pictures in the book. He's an artist."

"You can call me Ty. Now, who's ready to hear about a kitten called Frances?"

The kids raised their hands in unison, some waving their arms overhead.

Ty pushed the rocking chair aside and sat down on the rug at the head of the "class", his long legs folded under him yogi-style.

"Frances is a little ball of white fur," Ty began. He held up the open book in an outstretched arm so that the kids could see the pages. "She showed up one day on the deck of a man named Joe. Joe didn't know what to do with the little kitten with big blue eyes. He fed Frances a can of tuna."

A little girl in the back sang out, "My mom feeds our cats tuna, too."

"That's good to know. I guess Joe did the right thing. Thanks for sharing, Marsha," Ty said.

The kid tilted her head and grinned, preening under Ty's smile.

How does he know her name? Then Cass remembered his asking the kids' names as they had filed into the story corner. The man was more than impressive.

Usually, story hours freed Cass to work around the store, but the sound of his deep voice hypnotized her. She attempted to inventory a box of books that had been delivered that morning, but her eyes continued to stray from her computer screen to Ty.

"When Joe's niece Harper came to visit," Ty continued, "Frances decided that she wanted to live with Harper instead of Joe. So, Harper took Frances home with her and their great adventures began.

"Harper took Frances to school for show and tell, but Frances didn't like being in the classroom and ran out the door. All the children in Harper's class went looking for Frances and couldn't find her."

Turning the page, Ty rested the open book on his lap pausing the story. "Where do you think the children found Frances?"

He gazed at the group for a few beats waiting for someone to venture a guess, but no one uttered a sound. "She was with Mrs. O'Donnell the principal!"

Ty displayed the book again and read, "They found Frances sitting on the principal's desk lapping milk from a saucer while Mrs. O'Donnell sipped from a teacup."

The sweet chorus of children's laughter delighted

Cass. Ty laughed along with the kids.

"One day Harper's dad came home with tickets to the Carly Thomas concert," Ty read. "Harper was so excited. Frances wanted to go, too. But kittens don't go to concerts.

"Or do they? Harper's mom bought a big purse. Frances climbed right into the purse and went to the concert with Harper."

Ty paused frequently whenever a hand raised, listening, responding, laughing, taking his time with each child. They all followed along as he shared the adventures of Frances.

"Do you think that Frances really did get to meet Carly Thomas?" Lilly said from the back row. "She's my favorite singer, but tickets are too hard to get for her concerts. Besides, I don't think that a kitten could get into a concert."

"Can I tell you a secret?" Ty lowered his voice and leaned forward conspiratorially.

The kids reacted by leaning toward him ready to be let in on the secret.

"Don't tell anyone, but I have met Harper and Frances in real life. And it's the truth. Frances not only went to the concert, but she went backstage afterward and met Carly Thomas. Frances even got to go to the Grammy awards ceremony. Harper's daddy writes music, and he took Harper and Frances with him when he won an award."

The kids responded with a chorus of "wows."

He'll make a good dad someday. Cassidy arranged cookies on a large platter anticipating the conclusion of story hour.

The door opened and closed repeatedly as the

mothers entered the shop trailing the scents of perfume. Cassidy snickered taking in the women who had dropped off their kids wearing shorts, sweats and baggy T-shirts returning clad in form-fitting, pressed jeans, tight cotton sweaters and full makeup.

"The End." Ty closed the book.

The group burst into applause and then they left their seats and surrounded Ty. One little girl hugged him and then ran to her mom begging to buy the book.

****

Relieved that he hadn't embarrassed his sister-in-law, Ty stretched out his legs in front of him. He noticed a lone little boy seated in the story hour circle.

"What's up, Ethan? Didn't you like the story?'

The kid trained doleful eyes on Ty. "I really liked it."

"Aren't you going to get a book so I can sign it for you?"

The little boy's cheeks reddened. "Grandma said her check didn't come yet this month so I could come to the story hour, but I can't have a book. I came with Mrs. Procsal, Maddy's mom. Maddy is my best friend." He hung his head.

Ty didn't mean to embarrass the little boy and had to fix that. "Well, you're in luck, buddy."

He held up the book he had used to read to the children. "I bought this book for my niece and guess what?"

"What?"

"She already has one. So, I have an extra. Would you like it?"

Ethan still hadn't raised his head.

"You'd be doing me a big favor."

The kid trained puppy dog eyes on Ty. "Really?"

"Uh huh."

Ethan's face glowed with his wide smile as he sprang up and took the book from Ty.

"I can sign it if you want," Ty said.

"Yes, please. Thank you, Mister Ty."

Ty took a pen out of his back pocket and put Ethan's book on his lap. That didn't work, so he reached out and dragged one of the kids' miniature chairs in front of him, positioned it between his splayed legs and propped the book on the seat.

"I have never wanted to be a chair more in my life," Joelle whispered loudly to Cassidy.

Ty grinned and pulled the chair a little closer. Cassidy burst out laughing and drifted over behind him to look over his shoulder. He turned toward Joelle, chuckled and then bent his head over Ethan's book.

Wielding the pen rapidly on the inside cover of the book, he said, "What do you like to do, Ethan? Do you like any sports?"

"I like soccer."

Ty drew a soccer ball next to Frances the kitten, signed, "Happy Reading, Ty" on the title page, and handed Ethan the book.

"Wow," the little boy said, pie-eyed.

"This is awesome. Thank you so much." Ethan ran over to his best friend, Maddy, proudly displaying his prize.

Word spread among the kids that Ty wasn't providing just an ordinary autograph.

Cassie tapped Ty on the shoulder. "Want to move over to the alcove signing table? You'll be more comfortable."

"Sure." Ty rose to his feet.

Rina manned the register where the moms lined up to pay for copies of the book and Cassie positioned to Ty's right to take the receipts and to pass each open book to him for signing.

As their mothers finished their purchases, the kids queued up in front of Ty, holding their moms' hands and bubbling with excitement that they might receive a drawing of Frances. Ty asked each child what they most liked and then he drew Frances next to footballs, baseballs, dolls… anything the kids requested.

Then it was Ethan's friend Maddy's turn.

"Hi, Maddy. What do you like?" Ty said.

"I play the drums." She raised her shoulders shyly.

"Oh, that is *so* cool." Ty handed the book back to her.

Her face lit up when she saw the drum set that Ty had drawn next to Frances. "Thank you so much."

Maddy's mom leaned toward Ty. "Thank you for giving Ethan the book," she said softly.

"No problem." He glanced over at Ethan who hovered with Maddy by the plate of cookies. "What's his story?"

"His mom died last year so he had to move here to live with his grandma. His dad wasn't in the picture. They live across the street from me. Nice people. The community has been looking out for them."

"I'm part of the community now. If you ever need anything, please don't hesitate to call me."

"That's so kind of you. Thank you. I will."

The number of kids on the queue dwindled and slowly the bookstore emptied out. Rina was the last person in the line.

"Who's the book for?" Ty started to draw Frances.

"It's for me." Rina grinned at him.

"What do you like?"

Rina arched an eyebrow and Ty barked a laugh. "Now remember this is a children's book," he teased.

"I know. I like to read."

Ty finished her drawing and handed the book to her.

She hooted a laugh and then held the book out to show Cassidy. Ty had drawn Frances standing next to a stack of books. A closer look revealed one of the titles in the stack: *Fifty Shades of Grey.*

Ty shoved back his chair, strode over to the story corner, stacked the chairs in fours and carried them to the back storeroom. Heading toward the back of the shop with the last batch of chairs, he snatched one of the books off the signing table. After he stowed the chairs, he sat at Cassie's desk, autographed the book and then returned to the front of the store.

Rina stood next to Cass behind the register. Her gaze met Ty's as he approached. "I'm going to head home now. It was truly great meeting you, Ty. You certainly set the bar high for the next author who comes to do a book signing. I hope we get to see you again soon."

"Nice meeting you, too, Rina. I'm sure we will see each other again."

She bussed a kiss on Cassidy's cheek and left the store clutching her book.

"How did I do with my first and hopefully last book signing?" Ty put a book down on the counter in front of Cassidy.

"You were wonderful. I can't remember a more successful event here. The way you signed the book with an illustration was so special for each child. I can't thank you enough."

"I'm glad you're happy with how it went. I actually enjoyed myself." Ty slipped his wallet out of his back pocket, took out a black credit card and laid it on the counter. "I need to pay for two books."

"I saw what you did for Ethan. That was very kind of you. You don't have to pay for the book. I'll take care of it." She pushed his card towards him.

"Absolutely not. I want to pay for Ethan's book and for this one, too." He pushed the card back.

"Really, you don't have to."

"I insist."

Cassidy rang up the order.

"No need for a bag." He took back his credit card and slipped it into his wallet.

Ty leaned casually against the counter and inhaled her fresh honeysuckle scent. "Well, I guess I better get going. This was much more fun than I thought it would be. It was great meeting you. I hope we run into each other again sometime soon."

"I'd like that." She smiled. "Thank you again for filling in."

He pushed off the counter and headed toward the door.

"Wait a minute," she called.

Ty halted and turned toward her.

She rushed around the counter. "You forgot your book."

"That's not my book." He grinned at her. "It's yours."

Ty turned back around, walked out the door and waved his hand as he passed by the window.

****

43

Cassidy opened the book. On the inside cover he had drawn Cozy Nook Bookstore exactly. Frances sat in the front window looking outside. He had printed a phone number in the bottom corner and on the title page, *If you ever need me just call. See you soon, Ty.*

Cassidy closed the book and hugged it to her chest.

Chapter 6

Ty stood scrutinizing the canvas he worked on depicting three little girls twirling in the rain. He needed to add a few extra touches to the black and white painting, but he had run out of time. His brother, Kane, was on his way over with his niece, Harper. If Ty gave in to the temptation to keep working, he knew he would be lost for hours.

"One word, Ty, amazing."

Ty gave a start at his brother's booming voice from the doorway of the studio. "I didn't hear your truck pull up. Sorry. Hey, how did you get in?"

Kane set coffee house paper cups down on the table with Ty's brushes and paints. He dug a ring of keys out of his pocket and jingled them.

"You gave me a key when we were moving your stuff out of the condo." Kane fiddled with a key to take it off the ring.

"Keep it. I want you to have it."

The patter of footsteps interrupted their conversation. Harper dashed into the studio.

"Hi, Uncle Ty." Harper launched herself into Ty's arms.

He lifted her off the floor and twirled her around. "Hi, princess, I missed you."

"I missed you, too."

He set her back down gently and she gave him a hug.

"Daddy said I could go swimming in your lake. I have my bathing suit on under my dress." She tugged up the hem and showed him the neon pink one-piece suit.

"Are you sure you want to go swimming? The water is pretty cold," Ty said.

"I really do. I don't mind the cold. Daddy bought me a new unicorn floaty. He said you would blow it up for me."

Kane shrugged and Ty laughed at his brother's passing the buck. "No problem, kiddo. I have an air pump in the garage."

Harper turned her attention to the painting on the easel. "Uncle Ty when did you take that picture of my cousins?"

Kane crouched down to Harper's eye level. "It's not a picture, honey. Uncle Ty painted it."

"Really? Wow. It looks like a photo. I love it."

"Thanks, Harper. That's the best review I've had in a long time."

"I seriously doubt that," Kane said.

Ty shrugged his shoulders grinning at his twin.

Kane handed Ty a cup of coffee. The brothers fell into step following Harper who ran down the stairs full throttle. Ty made a trip to the garage for the air pump, grabbed two fluffy beach towels off the dryer in the laundry room, and then met Kane and Harper outside.

The sun had burned off morning clouds and the lake reflected the powder blue sky. The trio crossed the lawn that sloped to the water's edge toward the four green Adirondack chairs perched on the grass overlooking Redbird Lake.

Harper whipped off her dress, tossed it onto one of the chairs, and ran splashing into what had to be frigid water. Kane took off his shoes and stood ankle deep in the water while Ty blew up the float.

Kane sloshed forward until the water reached the hem of his shorts and then did a rapid about-face. "Brrr. Are you sure you want to go swimming? The water is freezing."

"It's not that cold." To prove it, Harper submerged and surfaced laughing.

Ty flung the unicorn raft into the water toward Harper.

"Thanks, Uncle Ty." The little girl scrambled aboard.

Kane left the water, dried his feet with a towel and then sat down next to Ty stretching out his long legs like his brother. "It really is beautiful here. I have to admit I thought you were crazy moving downstate away from Chicago. You're such a city guy. But I get it now. It's so peaceful."

"I love it here and I can drive to the city anytime I want. I like the community feel of the town, too. It's nice to go into the coffee shop and know everyone. I'm starting to feel like I belong." He stretched his arms up and locked his hands behind his head. "How is Mags feeling?"

"Much better. A little less morning sickness, although she's still pretty tired all the time." Kane's unwavering gaze locked on Harper.

Ty smiled at the love written all over his brother's face. Kane had changed when he had found out that he had a daughter. His sperm donation and Maggie's surrogacy for her sister who was married to Kane's best friend had brought Harper into the world after her intended parents had died in a plane crash. Kane had had no idea that he had a child during the first five years of her life. Fatherhood had Kane more relaxed and smiling.

He never thought about having children but seeing his brother with Harper, Ty started to think he wanted that, too. *Would Cassidy want children?* Glad that he hadn't voiced that premature and totally unlike him thought out loud, Ty continued to watch Harper's unbridled enjoyment swimming.

"Thanks again for stepping in at the book signing for Maggie. We haven't really had a chance to talk about it. How did it go? Was it uncomfortable for you?"

"No, it was great. The kids were fun, and I was happy to do it."

"The owner of the bookstore, Karen I think…"

"Cassidy," Ty interjected.

"Right. Cassidy called and asked Maggie how she was feeling the day after the event. Maggie thought that was so kind of her."

"She seemed like a very caring person. Did she say anything about me?"

"She said it went very well and they sold a lot of books." Kane turned towards Ty narrowing his eyes. "I don't know if she mentioned you…What am I missing here?"

Ty declined to answer and stared at the lake, apparently sparking a light bulb over Kane's head. "I get it. You liked the bookstore owner, didn't you?"

"I like a lot of people. Harper swims really well."

Kane wasn't swayed off subject by Ty's evasion. "I mean you *really* liked her, didn't you?"

Ty mulled over his answer. Would his brother think he was crazy that a week after meeting Cassidy, he still couldn't get her out of his mind? He dreamed about her.

Divided Heart

She was the first thing he thought of when he awoke each morning—completely out of character.

Truth was a must with Kane. His brother would see right through a lie. "Yeah. It's crazy, but I can't stop thinking about her."

"Crazy? Need I remind you that at the first sight of Maggie at the inn, I fell in love with her? It must be a twin thing. When we know, we know. So, what are you going to do?"

Ty rubbed his hands over his face. "I don't know yet."

Kane trained his eyes on Harper again. "I think that's enough swimming for now. Your lips are turning blue," he called out.

She gave a nod and started dragging the raft toward the shore.

"You know she's cold when she gives in without a fight," Kane said.

Ty squatted down holding a beach towel wide open. He wrapped Harper with the towel and then rubbed the sides of her arms briskly as she shivered under his hands. "Would you like a nice cup of hot cocoa? I have the cheese croissants you like and chocolate donuts, too."

Harper threw her arms around Ty's neck letting the towel fall to the ground. "I love you, Uncle Ty. You are the *best*."

She sprinted toward the house. The men followed behind her.

"So…When are you going to see Cassidy again?" Kane said.

"I don't have any plans. I'm hoping to run into her again in the coffee shop like I did the day of the book signing."

"Leaving it to chance? That doesn't sound like you. I have an idea. Harper was really disappointed that she missed the book signing with Maggie. Let's go to the bookstore after lunch so she can see the books on display."

"That's a great idea. Thanks."

****

Cassidy slit the tape on one of the boxes that the delivery driver had left outside by the back door of the shop. She had played catch up all morning since opening Cozy Nook Books late. The women's book club meeting the previous evening went longer than usual. Cass had regretted drinking the late-night coffee the minute her head had hit the pillow and caffeine prevented her falling asleep.

She wondered if Ty's ears had burned all night. His appearance at the book signing had monopolized most of the ladies' conversation. Cass also regretted that she had shown Rina Ty's autograph in her copy of *A Kitten Called Frances*. Rina had pestered her to call Ty with the number he had inscribed in the book. Although Cass couldn't bring herself to call him, she did look for him each morning at the coffee shop hoping to run into him again.

The sky darkened and an unpredicted rain shower pelted the front window. She turned on a few more lights around the store as the bookstore lived up to its name—cozy. The warm lighting beckoned her to curl up in one of the oversized chairs with a cup of tea and a book. But she had work to do. The phone rang just as she had stowed the last box of books in the storage room.

"Good afternoon, Cozy Nook Bookstore. This is Cassidy how may I help you?"

"You can help me by never letting me drink wine at a book club meeting again." Joelle groaned and Cassidy laughed. Joelle continued lamenting drinking herself into a hangover in Cassidy's ear. The front door whipped open.

A raven-haired little girl zipped inside and made a beeline for the table of books in the children's section.

Cassidy's breath caught in her throat. Joelle continued talking, but Cassidy didn't register what she said. Ty hurried through the door behind the child, a smile lighting his handsome face. He had cut his hair.

Hmm…I liked it longer.

"Daddy, please come here. I found it," the girl called out.

Without a word to Cassidy, Ty hurried toward his *daughter*?

Daddy? Did I hear right?

She couldn't catch her breath as if the man had flung a bucket of ice water at her. Ty was a father? He was married? Why hadn't he mentioned a wife and daughter?

"Hello. Are you there, Cassie?" Joelle yelled into her ear. "Cass are you all right?"

Cassidy snapped back to reality. "Oh…sorry. I'm fine. A customer just came in with his daughter, and I have to help them. I'll call you later."

"Are you sure you're okay?"

"Uh huh." She disconnected the call and scurried into the storage room to hide for a while. She needed a moment to compose herself.

How could she have misread Ty's signals? She thought he was as interested in her as she was in him.

But…in his defense, she had never asked about his personal life. She stiffened her posture and got ahold of herself.

With her emotions in check, she plastered a smile on her face and returned to the counter ready to deal with Ty and his daughter. The door opened again, and Ty walked in—again. Dimples creased his face with his wide smile. She gazed at Ty and then at the man standing by the little girl. And then back at Ty.

"Your hair is still long," she said.

He furrowed his brow, his blue eyes twinkling. "Well, yes, it is."

"I like it long." *What is wrong with me? Stop talking, Cassidy.* She bit her lip.

"That's good to know." Obviously amused, he said, "From the look on your face I might have forgotten to mention that I have an identical twin brother."

The child ran up to Ty with a book in hand. "Uncle Ty, would you please sign my book like you did at the book signing?"

"Of course I will, but first I want you to meet Miss Cassidy. She owns the store."

"Hi, Miss Cassidy, I really like your store. I like to read."

"Why thank you. You're in the right place." Cassidy was smitten with the black-haired little cutie. She had good manners and her addressing Ty as her uncle brought happy relief to Cass.

Ty took the book out of Harper's hands. "Cassidy, this is my niece, Harper." He paced toward the counter, scrounged a pen lying next to the computer and opened the book.

"Nice to meet you Harper," Cassidy said. "How do

you like having a book written about you?"

"The book is about Frances. I get to play a secondary character." Harper sighed. "That's what Mommy told me."

Her father stepped behind Harper. "Hi. I'm Kane, Ty's older brother."

"Older by a few minutes," Ty called over his shoulder as he continued to sign Harper's book.

Kane held out his hand to Cassidy and she accepted the handshake.

"I'm glad to meet you," Kane said. "My wife appreciated your call to see how she was feeling. I'm happy to say the morning sickness is starting to ease and she's slowly getting back to work on her next children's book."

"Is it another book about Frances?" Cassidy said.

"No. It's about our dog named Tornado. And he is really a tornado," Harper chimed in.

Ty's arm brushed Cassidy's when he handed the book back to Harper sending a sensual zing through her.

The little girl immediately opened the book to check out the autograph. "Oh look, Daddy! Uncle Ty drew Tornado next to Frances. Thank you Uncle Ty."

"You're very welcome, princess."

"I'm sorry to cut this visit short, Cassidy. But may I please pay for the book now?" Kane said. "We have to get on the road to miss the Chicago rush hour."

Kane handed Cassidy his credit card. Cassidy rang his order and then gave the credit card back to Kane. "We'll meet you back at the truck, Ty."

"I parked in the lot next to the store." Ty tossed a key fob to Kane. "I'll be right there."

"I look forward to seeing you again soon, Cassidy,"

Kane said.

"Me, too."

Harper took hold of Kane's hand. He ushered his daughter out of the store.

"I thought they'd never leave. Alone at last." Ty beamed at Cassidy. "Harper really wanted to see your display since she missed coming with Maggie. And I wanted a chance to see you again."

His admission had her heart racing and her cheeks flaming with a hot blush. His musky aftershave filled her senses. Everything about the man drew her to him.

"I wanted to see you again, too," she confessed. "And I'm very glad that you're not Harper's father."

"What? Why would you think that?"

"I was on the phone when Kane came in with Harper and I heard her call him Daddy and I thought he was you."

"Ah…It's not the first time we fooled someone." Ty chuckled. "Even though we weren't trying to fool you."

He took one of the store's business cards off of the counter. "I wish we had brought two cars, but I have to go. Is it okay if I give you a call sometime?"

She plucked the card out of his hand, wrote her cell phone number on the back and then handed it back. "I'd like that."

His face lit with a grin.

Oh. His smile would surely be her downfall.

Ty tucked the card in his wallet. "I better move."

She watched his retreat hoping that he'd call soon.

Chapter 7

Cassidy stalled outside the door fixating on the illuminated, red-lettered sign overhead: Cardinal Bar and Grill. She lingered on the sidewalk in the purpling twilight no longer convinced that she was up for the arranged date that evening with Rina's brother-in-law. Her best friend had repeatedly touted Jack's virtues in assuring Cass that he was a great catch. Good looking, nice, church going, a hard-working corporate rising star in his accounting or treasury or something like that job in Chicago, and ready to settle down and start a family.

When she had stood in front of her mirror at home dressed for the evening in white jeans and a summery blouse, she had pointed a finger at her reflection and declared, "You *will* have a nice time. And move on. Sawyer would want you to."

What a different story it was facing the moment that would lead her to take that notorious step to move on, even though Sawyer's dying wish was for her to find happiness again. She heaved a sigh, flung open the door and strode into the restaurant as if she wanted to be there.

The cover country band, the only act in town with gigs in that only bar in town, *The Billy Hills*, was setting up on the bar's makeshift stage as she approached the "front row" table where Rina, Mike and Jack chatted and laughed having the best time together.

What do they need me for? She almost turned tail

and ran.

But Rina caught sight of her. "Yay, you're here."

"Hello, Cassidy." Jack shoved back his chair, rose to his feet, and pulled out a vacant chair for her.

"Hi Jack. It's good to…" Although she finished her polite introduction, the band fired up and drowned out her last three words, "finally meet you."

She sat down and Jack slid her chair closer to the table.

"Hey, Cassie," Mickey said. "You look pretty tonight."

"I would say, beautiful is a better adjective." Jack beamed down at Cassidy before taking the seat opposite her.

"Thank you." She dipped her eyes to her lap as a wave of discomfort at the compliment washed over her.

Was he snowing her to win favor? Cass had no desire for empty compliments.

And then she met Jack's eyes across the table and detected only gentleness and kindness and genuine interest in her in their aqua depths. As billed, he was good looking in a fair-skinned, broil in the sun, pale-haired, Celtic way. Rina had asserted more than once in selling Cassidy on Jack that they would make beautiful babies together.

Hmm…

Cass might have agreed with her friend's gene pool predictions but for one thing—chemistry. She shouldn't have made snap judgments or comparisons, but when Sawyer had walked into her life, instant attraction had swamped her. Just as overwhelming, Ty Martin's simple gallantry when they had met in the coffee shop had spurred dreamy fantasy. Jack's pleasant face brought a smile to her lips, but a future that included baby making together? Nope.

Rina frowned as if she had read Cassidy's mind. "The music is so loud," she boomed.

"It is," Cass shouted back. "But I love this song. Don't you?"

"I like this band in general." Jack's bass voice projected over the music. "They played the last time that Mickey and I came here."

Rina and Cassidy chuckled in unison. Rina touched Jack's arm. "They'll play the next time you come, too. They're the only band in town."

"Well, you're lucky to have this caliber of musicians locally," Jack blasted. He picked up a pitcher of beer from the center of the table and faced Cass. "Can I pour you a mug?"

"Sure, thanks." She looked around the table. "Looks like I have some catching up to do."

The beer was flat. Cass had to focus *hard* to prevent her mood from matching her drink. The foursome gave up on screaming over the entertainment. While the band finished the first set, Cass sat in comfortable silence enjoying the music, grateful that she didn't have to make small talk. She had already run out.

At break, conversation around the table resumed. Jack asked about and pretended interest in Cassidy's store admitting that he'd never visited Cozy Nook Books, or any other bookstore, for that matter, since he never reads books.

Does Rina know this? If she did, surely, she'd recognize the game changer. Knowing Katherine Lynch, though, she would still defend the matchup reasoning that opposites attract, and that Jack was perfect for her.

Cassidy gamely tried to muster some enthusiasm listening to his enthusiastic job description, but numbers and ledgers and investments were her least favorite aspects of running her business. Her mom's, too. Cass was grateful that her mother had long since outsourced the store's accounting and that she didn't have to deal with that at all.

Neither Rina nor Mickey gave her any sign that the engineered date wasn't going swimmingly, but Cass inwardly started counting the minutes until she might make a socially acceptable exit. Her interest heightened when Mike and Jack reminisced about growing up together in the Chicago burbs and their family's forays into the big city to celebrate birthdays, summers on Navy Pier and during the holidays to see the lights and decorated department store windows. Cassidy loved Chicago and it was easy for her to add to the conversation.

The brothers' history during their teenage years explained why Cass hadn't met Jack until then. He had never lived in Redbird, unlike Mickey. The family moved downstate to Redbird when Jack was a freshman in high school leaving him in a military academy to "straighten" out. Hard to imagine the quiet, buttoned-down adult in front of her as a hellion.

The Billy Hills took the stage again and launched into a rendition of "Friends in Low Places." Billy, the lead singer imitated Garth Brooks well and Cass couldn't help grinning and tapping her foot in rhythm. When Jack asked her to dance, Cassidy snapped back to reality. She accepted only because he didn't deserve rudeness. Swaying loosely in Jack's arms, memories of love-struck dancing with Sawyer that first night after his book signing played in her mind—a stark comparison to how Jack made her feel.

Movement on the perimeter of the dance floor caught Cassidy's attention. Ty Martin sidled up to the bar, slid onto a stool and faced Johnny Kelly, the bartender, his handsome face a blurry reflection in the mirror behind the bar.

Her pulse quickened and butterflies fluttered in her chest. Jack's arms were not the arms she wanted around her in that moment. Cass tamped down the impulse to excuse herself, leave the dance floor, slip onto a bar stool next to Ty and turn her back on the going nowhere date. Were Ty leading her around the dance floor, Cass would have had far less reluctance taking that first step to move on that evening.

The song finished and Jack dropped his arms. "Another dance?"

"Um…" She stood in place, her back to the bar. Ty's presence behind her irresistibly attracted Cass as if she were a pole in his magnetic field.

Had he noticed her? What should she do? Certainly not just stand there with Jack hanging on her answer and all the other couples dancing around her.

"Can we please sit this one out, Jack? I'm a little tired from working all day."

"Of course, Cass." He placed a hand lightly on the small of her back and walked with her back to their table.

Cassidy forced herself to engage with Rina, Mickey and Jack not daring to even glance in Ty's direction. She sipped her warm beer, ate a couple of nachos, conversed in snatches over the din of music and acted like she didn't want to fly out the door. Which she did. Patting on Charlie's head on her sofa watching TV in her jammies never sounded so good.

Billy Hill's amplified voice boomed, "We have a treat for you tonight, folks. Everybody welcome Ty Martin on the keyboard."

What? Her eyes widened to saucers as she tracked Ty advancing to the stage. Sitting there in a front row table, her eyes riveted to his muscular body in motion made her feel like she had a spotlight on her to single out his attention. *Adoring fan in the audience, Ty, look this way.*

If he had noticed her, he gave no sign. He took a seat at the keyboard at stage left and focused on Billy, the bandleader.

Ty played the intro of the song, "Bench Love" cuing the rest of the band to play and Billy to sing the powerful lyrics that touched a swoony, romantic chord in Cassidy and probably every other female in the bar. When Ty harmonized with Billy, admiration of his surprising talent overwhelmed her.

"I love this song." Cass didn't take her eyes off the keyboardist.

"I can tell," Rina said drawing Cassidy's gaze.

Rina knew her too well to miss the sea change in Cass once Ty unknowingly insinuated into her date with Jack. Cassidy sensed that Rina read Jack's swan song in her eyes.

****

Cassidy's beautiful face was like a beacon in the audience. Ty had watched her dance with that guy reflected in the bar mirror trying to gauge her connection to the man and tamping down a surge of bitter jealousy. Since he had met her, he had fantasized about making an exclusive connection with her. Why hadn't he acted on pursuing her sooner? Was that guy competition?

On stage, he didn't need to look at the keyboard to play the melody his brother, Kane, had composed, so he ventured a glance out at the tables. His gaze met and locked directly on Cassidy's eyes. They smiled at each other as if no one else were in the place. Ty sang the refrain duetting with his pal, Billy as if serenading Cassidy with the love song.

"One more number with us, Ty?" Billy said after the applause died down.

"Sure. What do you have in mind?"

" 'Take Me Home With You Tonight.' "

Ty gave Billy a nod, once again singing the lyrics to her beaming face wishing that she would take *him* home with her that night.

Rina and her husband, Ty assumed, took the dance floor, but Cassidy didn't leave her seat. Nor did she unlock her gaze from his to turn her attention to the man across from her. A good sign? He thought, yes.

At the end of the number, Ty's performance repertoire was exhausted. Billy thanked him at the mic and Ty left the stage returning to his seat at the bar.

"Great job," the bartender said. "You can really play, man."

"Thanks, Johnny. Piano lessons when I was a kid. Unlike my twin brother who was a natural. He wrote both those songs."

"H. Binder Martin is your brother?"

"Yep." Ty drained his beer mug.

"I'm impressed. Want another of those?"

"Sure. Why not?" Ty handed the mug to Johnny and then searched out Cassidy's reflection in the mirror.

She had left the table. Rina and the two men

remained in place. A purse hung over the back of the vacant chair. Ty figured she hadn't left the restaurant entirely. Maybe a trip to the ladies' room.

"I'll be right back. Visiting the facilities."

Johnny nodded his head.

The washrooms were situated down a narrow corridor which was empty. The door with the stencil of a female outline was first on the right. Although the music was muted there, the floorboards beneath his boots vibrated with the bass and the yeasty smell of beer permeated the air. Ty debated hanging out in the hall on the chance that he might encounter Cass leaving the washroom. But would he come off as a stalker?

He was about to pass by the ladies' room when the door swung open, and Cassidy appeared.

"Oh." She halted in the threshold and the door came to rest against her right shoulder. "Hi."

"Hi yourself. You look lovely tonight, Cassidy."

She brought a hand to her cheek. "Thank you. That's so nice of you to say. You were amazing up there. A celebrated artist? A musician? Wow, Ty."

He huffed a laugh, wagging his head. "Hardly a musician. That's my brother Kane all the way. But I guess you could say I've learned a thing or two at my twin's knee."

"I'll say. Truly, I enjoyed listening to you sing."

"Thanks. Well…" Ask her out on a date? Tell her he wished that she'd take him home with her tonight having sung the song to her?

"Yes, well…"

They hung in each other's thrall a few moments.

"I guess I better get back to the table," she said.

"Of course."

"See you, Ty."

"Yes. See you, Cassidy."

Chapter 8

Ty swept his soaking wet T-shirt over his head and draped it over the deck rail. A breeze ruffled his hair and cooled the sweat on his forehead. He plopped down into an Adirondack chair and guzzled a bottle of water. The view of the sunrise over the glistening water brought peace and the jog he had taken around the lake had helped to clear the cobwebs from his sleep-deprived brain. He had tossed and turned all night thinking of Cassidy and her date. It had taken maximum control not to stride over to her table the night before and ask her to dance.

He closed his eyes and was transported back to the bar in his mind. Was she serious about the guy? His gut told him that they weren't a couple—not with the way she had gazed at him when he was on stage with the band. He was done wondering. With a rudimentary plan in mind, Ty went into the house to take a shower, detouring in the kitchen to snatch his cell phone off the charger and check messages.

The phone rang in his hand, and he answered without looking at the number.

"Hey big dog, how's it hanging?" came his college buddy's unmistakable bass voice.

"Hunter, it's been a while. Where are you?"

"I landed at Midway last night. I'm staying at Dryden's place in the Sterling, close to your condo."

"I'm not renting the condo anymore."

He let out a belly laugh. "Did Kane finally throw you out?"

"No, even though once Maggie came into his life I'm sure he thought about it. I bought a house at Redbird Lake downstate."

Hunter snorted. "Ty leaving the city, has hell frozen over? But seriously how does Melanie feel about leaving the city?"

"Melanie was long gone before I bought the place."

"You are so much better off without her."

Couldn't agree more. "I thought you weren't coming to Chicago until next month. What's up?"

"Drum roll please…" Hunter chuckled. "I'm meeting with my publisher."

"Congratulations, that's amazing! But I'm not surprised. I told you your book was great."

"I have you to thank for pushing me and for giving me the idea for a series."

"No thanks needed. But when you go on your book tour I know a bookstore you need to visit."

"It's a deal. I have to run, buddy but I want to see you before I head back to California. You, Bubba, and Dryden, we have to get together, maybe this weekend?"

"Sounds great, I'll call you tonight and we'll plan something." Ty smiled as he plugged his phone back into the charger and climbed the stairs to shower and change.

Ty, Bubba, Dryden and Hunter, the Bama Boys. They met the first day of baseball practice at University of Alabama, hit it off immediately and were inseparable for four years. Full of confidence and a dose of cockiness, the foursome helped the team qualify for the national championship each year and in their senior year they took home the trophy. A picture of Ty's walk off, grand slam homerun appeared in *Sports Illustrated* along with a picture of the Bama boys. He looked forward to seeing them again.

After his shower he checked his email and scheduled a time for the gallery to pick up the remaining pieces for his upcoming show. Business done, he headed out to his truck to work his plan for a date with Cassidy.

He walked three blocks to Coffee & More, since closer parking spaces were unavailable. The line of customers at the only breakfast spot in town snaked out the door. Ty had never seen the line that long. Jeannie, the predictably snarky waitress, bumped into him from behind and stumbled rushing toward the door. Ty shot his arm out and prevented her from hitting the ground.

"Hey Jeanie. Are you okay?" He kept his arm around her until she was steady on her feet.

"The damn car wouldn't start this morning," she barked.

But then a smile bloomed on her face. "Won't your girlfriend be jealous that you're hugging me out here in public?"

"I don't have a girlfriend." He released her gently.

"Good news for the ladies in town. Good grief, Mirela is going to have my head." She bent to pick up her purse that had fallen off her shoulder when she stumbled.

"Is there anything I can do to help?"

Jeannie gaped him. "Do you mean that?"

"I never say anything I don't mean."

"Then come on." She grabbed his hand and towed him to the back door of the restaurant into the kitchen.

"Charlene this is Ty. Ty this is Charlene," she said

to the apron-clad cook. "He's here to help out this morning."

"Morning," Charlene grunted without raising her eyes from the griddle.

"Nice to meet you," Ty said.

Jeannie stowed her purse in the back office, grabbed an apron, tied it around her waist, threw an apron to Ty and then sashayed out the swinging doors to face Mirela and the clamoring customers.

With no apparent time for courtesy, Charlene put him to work on the spot. He filled coffee mugs, set them on a tray and brought caffeine fixes out to the grumbling customers. He apologized for the wait, owning the turmoil as if he worked at the restaurant. His pleasant demeanor calmed the madding crowd.

Ty wasn't a complete stranger to serving food. He had worked summers at his mom's bakery and knew his way around a kitchen. After he had distributed coffee, he cooked bacon, wrapped sandwiches for takeout, toasted bread, loaded the dishwasher and filled coffee pots. Rapidly, the crowd thinned, and the line disappeared. He mopped his sweaty face with a paper towel and gladly accepted the glass of ice water that Charlene offered him.

"Thanks for the help. How long have you worked in a restaurant?" she said.

Ty glanced at the clock on the wall. "I guess about two hours."

Charlene widened her eyes. "Wow, I'm impressed. You were very efficient."

"I've never worked in a restaurant before, but I've worked in my mom's bakery. Jeannie was upset that she was running late, and I offered to help. No big deal."

"No big deal?" Jeannie barged through the doors. "It

certainly *is* a big deal. You are as nice as people around town have said about you."

"People have been talking about me? Why?"

"Everyone talked about you for days after the book signing at Cozy Nook. You made a huge hit with the kids… and the moms too." She waggled her eyebrows.

Ty laughed at her innuendo. "I better get going." He untied the apron and handed it to Jeannie.

"Thanks, Ty. I really appreciate your help."

"My pleasure." He left the kitchen and stood at the counter. Mirela bustled right over to him.

"What do you need Ty?"

"Maybe you can give me some insider info, Mirela? I know that Cassidy from the bookstore comes in here in the mornings. What does she buy? Coffee? Tea?"

"Her usual is a hot tea with lemon and one teaspoon of sugar."

"I'm on my way to the bookstore. Can I please have a black coffee and a hot tea with lemon and one teaspoon of sugar, please?"

She winked at him and then prepared his drinks.

****

Cassidy taped the bottom of the last cardboard box and added it to the line of open boxes on the tabletop. The office printer spat out invoices and labels. Her online business had taken off. Cass even considered hiring some part-time help for the remainder of the summer to handle order volume. She had pulled the books and stacked them next to the boxes matched to ordered titles and quantities.

Her mother had fought implementing online shopping for years, but Sawyer had used his considerable charm to convince her that it would be a success. He had proven that he was right when his book, the first offered for sale on the newly developed Cozy Nook Bookstore's website, constantly sold out. He had autographed boxes of books before he had fallen sick. Sadly, other than one copy Cass had saved for herself, the supply of signed books had long since depleted. Even so, the book still sold, and she had to reorder frequently.

She picked his book off the top of a pile. Tears brimmed. *Through My Lens* had hit the New York Times Bestseller list and had remained there for months after publication. Sawyer was proud of the achievement, and she had overflowed with pride for Sawyer. Cassidy strongly felt his presence when she came into the store each morning. Some days, like that morning, she swore that she smelled his aftershave. On bad days she talked to him and felt his love encompass her.

She opened the book and gasped reading the title page. Sawyer's trademark signature, "See the world through your own lens, Sawyer", was clearly written on the page.

One by one, she checked his books in the waiting-to-ship stack. Sawyer's autograph was there in each copy.

How is this possible? Then it occurred to her. She knew in her heart that Sawyer somehow remained there where they had first met so he might still take care of her.

"Thank you. I love you," she whispered.

The bell on the store's front door jangled. Cassidy swiped away the tears beneath her eyes. Forcing a smile, she turned towards the door. Ty approached her beaming and bearing gifts from Coffee & More.

"Good morning." He placed a hot beverage cup on

the counter in front of her.

"What a nice surprise." She took a tentative sip. "Delish. How did you know my favorite drink?"

"I asked Mirela. What's all this?" He pointed to the "shipping" table.

"Online orders I have to get out today."

He drifted over to the table, picked up a copy of *Through My Lens,* and browsed through it.

"These photographs are amazing," he murmured. He continued to turn the pages.

Ty closed the book and read the author's name out loud, "Sawyer Finnegan. Your husband?"

"Yes. We met here when he launched this book."

"Beautiful work. He was a true artist." He placed the book back on the stack and brushed her hand. "Do you need any help sealing boxes? I'm pretty good with a tape gun."

He grabbed the tape gun and pretended to shoot at the boxes, but the tape caught on his hand streaming out a long length of stickiness. The silliness broke Cassidy's somber mood and she smiled. Ty regrouped and taped all the boxes neatly while Cassidy affixed the labels making quick work of finishing the task.

"I think I'm crazy, but do you smell bacon?" Cassidy set the last box on the floor next to the counter for the carrier's pickup.

Ty looked down at the front of his shirt. Splatters of grease and other stains dotted the once crisp, spotless linen. "I'm pretty sure you smell me."

"Well, that's an interesting choice of cologne," Cassidy teased.

Ty filled her in on how he had spent his morning.

My goodness, Ty seems too good to be true. Helping

out Jeannie and now helping me.

"I planned on bringing you one of Charlene's amazing blueberry muffins to go with your tea, but they were gone by the time the crowd thinned."

"They really are the best I have ever tasted."

"Truth is, I stopped by because I wanted to see you again after last night. I noticed your hours posted on the front door. It says you close from 1:30 to 2:30 for lunch. If you don't have any plans today would you like to go to lunch with me?"

"My stomach is grumbling just thinking about Charlene's muffins and right now bacon, too. I would love to go to lunch with you. But you have to let me treat to thank you for helping me this morning."

"I only taped a few boxes, and my mother would kill me if I let a woman pay on a date." He checked his watch. "I'll be back in an hour to pick you up. I promise not to smell like bacon."

Ty tossed his empty cup in the waste bin next to the counter and turned toward the door.

Cassidy watched him leave and waved back at him through the window.

For the first time since losing Sawyer, she looked forward to spending time in another man's company. She closed her eyes and knew Sawyer was smiling.

Chapter 9

The Cardinal Bar and Grill had a different vibe in the daytime—more a soda pop and burgers, kids-friendly restaurant than a beer on tap singles and date night, country bar. Ty ushered Cassidy past the empty bar stools toward the back of the restaurant eyeing the nearby clientele. He pointed toward a booth furthest away from a family table where two elementary school aged boys duked it out blowing straw wrappers at each other while their parents dug into their lunches pointedly ignoring the kids and each other.

Ty slid into the booth opposite Cass rewarded by her radiant smile across the table.

"This is a nice treat," she said. "I never leave the store for lunch."

She huffed a laugh. "Actually, I usually forget to eat lunch entirely. What do you think you'll order?"

"I've probably had every sandwich on the menu by now. I think a burger and fries. You?"

"That sounds good to me."

He scanned the room searching for a waiter. None in sight. "Hang on a minute. I'll go put in our order."

Ty stepped up to the bar. "Hey, Johnny. How are you today?"

"Good. What can I do for you?"

"Can I put in an order for a couple of burgers and fries?"

"Sure. Something to drink?"

"Cass?" Ty called out to Cassidy. "Want something to drink?"

"Iced tea, please?" came her reply.

"Got it," Johnny said.

"I'm good with water. Thanks, Johnny."

"Okay we're set." Ty settled into his seat on the cardinal red, vinyl upholstered bench.

His gaze was drawn to Cassidy's beautiful face and sparkling emerald eyes. "Have I told you that you look beautiful today?"

"No, you didn't." Her fair cheeks reddened but she didn't drop her gaze.

He reached across the table and gently clasped her hand still training his gaze into her eyes. "Well, you do. *Very* beautiful."

She touched her free hand to the side of her face. "Thank you, Ty. You look pretty good yourself."

"That's nice to hear, thanks." He gave her hand a squeeze gratified that she didn't draw away. "I haven't been able to get you out of mind, Cass since the first time I saw you at the coffee shop."

A slow smile bloomed on her lips and her eyes sparkled. "The same for me."

That the powerful attraction was mutual brought encouragement and relief. He didn't know what he'd do if she hadn't said that he at least had a chance to win her over that guy he had seen her with there. Or any other competition.

But she didn't have to tell him that although seemingly available, she was fragile and vulnerable. He'd have to move cautiously even though he wanted to race into her life and enfold her into his. Ty wanted to know everything about the woman. He had never felt that way before and he didn't want to blow it by making her feel interrogated or pressured. But he did have one pressing question.

"Are you dating that guy I saw you with here the other night?"

"Oh." She tucked a tendril of hair behind her ear. "No. I mean yes," Cass stammered.

Ty arched his eyebrows. "Yes?"

"I mean, yes, it was a date. A fixup actually. Jack is Rina's brother-in-law."

"A first date?"

"Yes. A first meeting date." Her eyes softened, the prettiest shade of sea green. "And the last date with Jack. He's a really nice person but I don't see anything beyond friendship with him."

"Good. I'm good then."

Her lips twisted and her eyes narrowed. "Just to be clear. You're good about what?"

"I'm good to ask you to date me."

Cass chuckled. "Well, that's direct."

"No better way to be. Are you interested?"

"Interested, yes." Her eyes bored into his. "Ready? That's another story. I *think* I'm ready. I'm trying to be."

Johnny brought their order to the table himself and then left them to eat their lunch. The barbecue aroma of grilled meat tempted Ty to wolf down the burger, but he didn't take a bite. He wanted to linger there in her company as long as she was willing to stay with him— all day, all night. Surprising to him, he fantasized about having her in his company every day and night.

She removed the top bun from her sandwich and wielded the ketchup bottle.

"Want some?" Cass held out the red plastic bottle. Apparently everything in the Cardinal Bar and Grill was red.

Ty added the condiment to his sandwich and then took a gratifying bite of the hearty, just the right amount of greasy meat.

"Tell me more about your family, Ty?"

"What would you like to know?"

Cass regarded him expectantly. "You have a big family, right?"

"I do. My immediate family is pretty big and add in the extended family, which is growing baby by baby, you get epic reunions."

"Sounds like such fun. What was it like growing up?"

"Hmm…" He paused considering how to frame the unique history of the Binder-Martin's.

Should I tell her about the Legend of the Three Butterflies and the Sacred Source-given powers identical triplets through my family's generations possess? How about my Aunt Kay is a walking crystal ball? Or my cousin Skye talks to maritime creatures and can turn herself and others into dolphins, pelicans, whales…And then there are my toddler nieces. Last I heard they turned themselves into pygmy ponies.

Ty had always believed that the creative talents, including his own, that ran along his family lines owed to the Sacred Source, too. But only the first born, identical female triplets through the ages inherited the fullest powers. Best to relate the more mundane aspects of his more than vibrant family life.

"Since I'm an identical twin, I was never lonely as a kid, and sibling rivalry between me and Kane really never existed except to razz each other now as adults. My sister is the eldest in the family and has always been the little mommy to me and Kane and my two other brothers. She's the first to have a baby, too. My niece, Meadow, is in first grade now. You met Kane at the bookstore and he's soon to be the father of two."

He bit back a smile intending to tell her about his and Kane's full names. Ty had always thought that the difficult time their tiny mother had carrying two eight-pound twins in pregnancy and her extended labor and delivery giving them birth had left her crazed when it came to naming her babies.

Ty smiled broadly.

"What are you smiling about?" Cass's eyes crinkled with her grin apparently wanting to get in on the joke.

"My name, Ty, and Kane's are nicknames."

"Okay," she said. "Ty for Tyler? I can't think of a proper name for Kane." She sipped on the straw in her tall glass.

"His full name is Hurrikane, spelled like the noun except with a k instead of a c."

Cassidy snorted a laugh clapping a hand over her nose and mouth. "Oh my gosh, I think tea came out my nose!

"And your birth name is?" she managed.

"Typhoon."

She threw back her head with a burst of giggles. He waited for her laughter to subside. He was tempted to time it, it went on for so long. Cass took a deep breath and then met his gaze, her eyes streaming gleeful tears. He grinned back at her which set her off giggling again.

"Whatever you do, don't take another bite of burger. I don't want to have to use the Heimlich maneuver on you."

"Oh, good grief." She wrapped her arms around her waist and guffawed.

"And…" she struggled to collect herself. "Didn't Harper tell me that they have a dog…"

Cass snorted. "A dog named…" She squeaked another gleeful laugh. "Tornado?"

"Uh huh."

"Oh my gosh." She swiped tears away from beneath her eyes with a napkin. "I can't wait to meet your mom. Promise me I'll get to."

Nothing would please him more. "You've got it, pretty lady. So, you're an only child. I would imagine you had a far more peaceful childhood than I did."

"I guess so. I had a wonderful childhood. I wish you could have met both my parents. Now that you live in Redbird, I'm sure you'll hear about them from neighbors. They were so loved by the community. My dad, who died when he was only forty-six years old of leukemia, was the town paint contractor. His truck was probably parked in every single driveway in town at one time or another. Rina's husband, Mickey apprenticed with Daddy when he was in high school and he inherited the business, Corrigan's Painting, still in operation today, when dad learned that his disease was terminal."

"Your dad didn't want your mom or you to inherit it?"

"Oh no. It never occurred to mom, and I was still in college when he died. Mickey deserved it. Plus, my mother had a thriving business with the bookstore. They never really talked finances to me, but I'll bet that she was the primary bread winner in my family. She was the dearest, sweetest, smartest woman."

"Like her daughter."

"Oh." She gave him a wistful smile. "I'd love to think I take after either of my parents. They were very special."

"I'm sure they were, having raised you. Is it hard for you…" Ty hesitated to ask her about her husband.

He knew that more than a year had passed since he had died. Were the wounds still too fresh? Would his prying wipe that soft smile from her face?

Cass narrowed her eyes and tilted her head. "You're curious about Sawyer, right?" she intuited.

"Only if you want to talk about him. I would never want to cause you unnecessary grief, Cass."

"He was everything to me and we were so happy together. Even during his terrible illness, he brought me joy. When he died, I honestly didn't think I could go on without him." She lowered her eyes and wagged her head.

Guilt pinched in Ty's gut having inadvertently uncapped her well of sorrow. He reached across the table and clasped her hands gently. "I'm sorry I asked, Cass. But look at you now running your mom's store so successfully surrounded by people who love you."

He took her thin smile as a good sign.

"I *am* happy living and working here," she said.

"And now you've met me."

"That's true." Cass pursed her lips, amusement dancing in her eyes.

She eyed their linked hands, and he picked up on the cue to let go. Cass raised her head and gazed directly into his eyes.

"We should finish lunch so you can reopen the bookstore," Ty said.

"Yes, we should." She didn't tear her gaze away from his face or pick up her hamburger to eat.

"Our lunch has probably gone cold."

"I'm sure it has. But I can eat burgers cold."

"Me, too."

Her penetrating gaze didn't unnerve him. The opposite. Despite that she remained a grieving widow, attraction sizzled between them like a live wire. Moments passed locked in each other's gazes before they resumed eating their lunches.

While he ate, Ty mulled over his next move. Could he take her to dinner that night? Too eager? Too soon? Would he wind up in the friend zone like first date, fixup Jack if he pressed too hard and fast?

He deferred asking her out again on the spot, deciding instead to pay the bill and walk her back to Cozy Nook Books.

The weather was unusually mild and pleasant for July in southern Illinois, and he enjoyed the light breeze walking with a pretty woman on a pretty summer's day. Cass worked the key in the lock, shoved the store's front door partially open and then turned in the threshold to face him.

"Thank you so much for lunch."

"You're welcome. I was wondering. Are you free for dinner tomorrow evening?"

She knit her brows. "I'd love to say yes, but I can't. I'm running a charity softball game tomorrow. It starts after work, so dinners afterward are just grab and go."

"Okay. How about Saturday, then?"

Cass gifted him with a smile. "Yes, thank you. I'd love to have dinner with you."

He pecked a kiss on her lips. "See you Saturday. I'll

text later with details."

"Sounds good. Say…" She eyed the muscles in his arms. "Any interest in playing for my side in the game tomorrow? Do you play softball?"

The memory of the *Sports Illustrated* article about his grand slam in the Nationals and Bama Boys notoriety flashed in his mind. "Yes, you could say that."

"Want to come? It's at Memorial Field at 5:30."

"I'll be there, Cass. See you tomorrow. Might even bring a few buddies if they're available."

"That would be great. Thanks, Ty."

Chapter 10

Cassidy raced through her front door. "Charlie!" she shouted.

She felt guilty having neglected her dog so long late in the day. She had gotten hung up with late arrival customers at the bookstore delaying her feeding and walking Charlie, changing into softball gear and standing on her front step on time for Joelle's lift to the field.

Charlie lumbered down the stairs and stopped at her feet.

"Were you in my bed sleeping all day, lazy? There's my good boy." She bent down and scratched his ears.

"Let's go for a walk and I'll fix your dinner."

A walk up and down the block sufficed after Charlie's long wait to relieve himself. Next she put down his dinner bowl on the floor and then sped up the stairs yanking her shirt off over her head, her heart pumping, both with the need for speed and nervous anticipation of seeing Ty.

She hadn't thought he'd accept playing with the locals. The bookstore sponsored the game to raise money for a free lunch program at the local elementary and high schools. Joelle spearheaded the fundraiser. Her children attended the elementary school. At a joint PTA meeting she was shocked at how many families had a hard time paying for lunches. Joelle jumped in and convinced the

PTA mothers and the teachers at both schools to sign up to compete in a fun game to raise money for the new program.

Cassidy changed into bike shorts and a Redbird Bulldog T-shirt. She took a few seconds to swipe a coat of mascara on her lashes and a quick touch up of lipstick before zooming downstairs and out the door. Joelle turned into the driveway as the door latched behind Cass.

She jumped into the sleek convertible breathing heavily. Cass took a scrunchie off her wrist and wound it around her hair securing a ponytail.

"Why do you have Keith's car?" Cass checked her reflection in the visor mirror.

"It's his weekend to have the kids. He likes to take the minivan, and I'm not going to lie. I love driving the Benz."

"The kids will be sorry to miss the game."

"They'll be there. Keith and Travis are bringing them to the game," Joelle said in a nonchalant tone.

Joelle and her husband had divorced two years ago because he had fallen in love with a man. Cassidy was so proud of her friend for the way she had weathered the storm of her husband's leaving. Joelle and Keith put the children first and remained friends.

They pulled into the parking lot in back of the field. Joelle popped the trunk, and they began hoisting equipment and boxes filled with supplies. Mickey and Rina jogged over to help. Hugs exchanged and the foursome made their way to the PTA's dugout. The teacher's team practiced on the field. The lineup of coaches and male teachers intimidated Cassidy. The PTA team boasted mostly petite mothers and one unlucky male so far—Mickey.

"What did I get us into?" Joelle grimaced.

"Rina and I played high school ball. It will be all right—I hope," Cassidy said.

She and Joelle set up a table of baked goods and snacks. Mickey and Rina had brought two coolers filled with drinks. The stands started to fill with families.

"Do we even have enough people for a team?" Joelle's gaze swept the field side to side from dugout to dugout. The showing on the PTA side was paltry while the teacher dugout was full capacity.

"We'll be fine. Ty's coming and he said something about bringing his buddies."

"Hope he gets here soon. Bobby Big Balls, is rallying his team and wants to get the game started."

Cassidy barked a laugh at Joelle's nickname for the high school baseball coach.

She threaded her pony tail through the back of a baseball cap and then turned at the sound of an engine roar behind her. A shiny black Ford 150 barreled into the lot lurching to a stop. Four doors flew open. Ty and three tall hunks, mitts in hand, jumped out and strode towards Cassidy and Joelle.

"I told you he would come." Cassidy said her heart winging.

"Is it me or are they walking in slow motion?" Joelle said. "Do you hear music? I swear I hear the theme from *Top Gun*. Damn. Look at those studs."

Cassidy's gaze locked only on Ty, her pulse accelerating. He wore a University of Alabama baseball cap, his black hair curling around the edges. Her fingers itched to run through the curls. A tight black T-shirt grabbed the muscles on his arms and stretched tight over his chest defining washboard abs. The shirt that was tucked into low slung cargo shorts hiked up with his wave exposing a ribbon of man-v skin. Cassidy felt a tightening in her core that she hadn't felt in a long time.

"I'm sorry we're late. Hunter got stuck in traffic on the rural route. These are the boys, Bubba, Hunter and Dryden. Guys, these lovely ladies are Cassidy and Joelle," Ty said.

They shook hands and then they joined the PTA team in the dugout. Mickey held out the roster with questions in his eyes. Cassidy supplied the names for him to add to the players list.

"Better get going before Bobby Big Balls has a coronary," Joelle quipped.

Ty laughed so hard he looked like he'd choke.

Cassidy supplied him with a bottle of water which he guzzled. "Unflattering nickname for the coach, but I think you'll see it's right on."

"Love Joelle's sense of humor."

"Me, too. Thanks for coming. You're really saving the day. We looked like the Bad News Bears before you all showed up."

He leaned down and kissed her cheek. "I'll take any opportunity to be with you."

Nervousness evaporated. Ty made her feel desirable…and confident.

Mickey called her name. She picked up a bat, winked at Ty and then sashayed to home plate.

****

"Now *that* is hot." Hunter's voice echoed throughout the dugout.

"Watch it." Ty couldn't take his eyes off Cassidy's bouncing blonde ponytail, curves into a narrow waistline and swaying hips hugged perfectly by tight spandex. As his mom would say, he was smitten and he agreed with Hunter. She was smoking hot.

Cassidy hadn't yet set her stance before the baseball coach on the mound with the fitting nickname threw a pitch that barely missed hitting her.

Ty stood up and walked to the end of the dugout, curling his fingers around the chain link fence. "What the hell is he doing? This is a charity game for fun right?"

Rina came to stand next to him. "He's just mad. We went to school with him—a local boy through and through. Cassidy turned Bob down in high school every time he asked her out. After Sawyer died he tried to make a move again and she shot him down." Rina laughed. "Don't worry about Cass, she can hold her own."

Cassidy whacked the next pitch straight to the mound. The hit would have clocked Bob's head if he hadn't ducked. She made it safe to first base. Ty jogged over and high fived her.

The PTA scored one run before the third out without Ty and his buddies entering into the batting order. Instead, they took the field to shore up the defense.

Cassidy played first base, Rina pitched, and Joelle took up the short stop position. Dryden played second base, Hunter covered third and Bubba and Ty joined a woman in the outfield. The teachers' team was strong, but the PTA managed to hold them to one run tying the game. Ty made a diving catch of Bob's line drive for the third out. Bob slammed his bat down on the ground.

"Nice hit." Ty passed Bob walking off the field.

"Lucky catch," Bob barked. He stormed to the mound.

Ty held his tongue. He refused to engage in a pissing

contest with the blowhard. He would not embarrass himself or make Cassidy regret inviting him.

After a few more innings locked in a tie, the ump, a high school kid who had called the game so far without a shred of bias, agreed to a break so the PTA could raise funds.

Cassidy held up a raffle ticket spool and a bucket in front of Ty. She pointed to another ticket wheel and bucket on the bench. "Want to help me sell 50/50s in the stands?"

"Sure." He grabbed the tickets and bucket and followed her to the opposing team's side of the field.

He enjoyed meeting townspeople, teasing the women and cajoling the men into buying tickets. The bucket filled with money and ticket stubs for the drawing. Familiar faces of kids and moms from the book signing beamed at him from his team's stands.

His little pal, Ethan, sat by himself on the top bleacher. Ty tore off a long line of tickets and climbed up the bleachers to the top bench.

"Hi, Ethan. Good to see you, buddy."

"Hi, Mister Ty." He gifted him a bright smile.

"Are you here by yourself?"

"I rode my bike." He pointed over his shoulder. "My grandma's house is up that road. Grandma is walking to the field."

"Will you do me a favor?"

"Sure."

"It winds up I didn't know that since I'm a seller, I'm not allowed to buy raffle tickets for myself, but I did before I learned the rule. Will you please take these off my hands, so I don't get in trouble?"

"Wow. Sure, I will."

He handed Ethan about twenty tickets. "If you win, you have to promise me something."

"What?"

"You have to treat yourself and your grandma to ice cream with your winnings. Can you do that?"

"I can. Thanks, Mister Ty.

He smiled making his way back down to ground level where Cassidy waited for him. "Mr. Martin, sometimes I wonder if you're for real. Are you truly this nice?"

Ty was about to answer her when Bob bellowed, "Break over," cutting him short.

"If by nice you mean do I truly care about people? Then yes, I'm always nice. If you're asking do I want to be nice to *Bob* right now, then no. I want to punch him nicely in the face."

Cassidy snorted a laugh, clasped his hand and tugged him toward the dugout.

The tie score didn't break into the top of the ninth, PTA team at bat. Ty asked Mickey if he could pinch hit for Joelle.

"My leg is killing me," Joelle piped up from the bench.

"Which leg is it?" Dryden said, apparently more than interested in the woman judging from the concerned expression on his face.

"Whichever one it has to be so I can sit this one out and let Ty hit. I'd rather that he batted the last out, not me." Joelle gave him a crooked smile.

Dryden chuckled. "Darlin', you don't know Ty."

Mickey made the substitution in the batting order because of injury and Ty strolled to the plate. Bob kicked around on the mound like a mad bull. He wound up and pitched a hard curve ball grazing Ty's shoulder. Bob's smirk infuriated Ty.

Ty turned to the ump. "I don't want the walk," he said under his breath.

The kid yelled, "Foul ball."

"What?" Bob yelled back.

"It hit the tip of my bat." Ty said staring the pitcher down.

"Bullshit."

"There are kids here, man. Watch the language."

The hit stung, but he wasn't about to clue Bob in. Ty rolled his shoulder a few times and then positioned his bat, squinted and locked his eyes on Bob's every move.

"Oh boy." Dryden jumped off the bench and stood at the opening of the dugout.

Bubba and Hunter rose to join him.

"He poked the bear," Hunter said.

"It's show time," Bubba yelled.

Ty turned toward the dugout, pointed his bat to center field and then winked at Cassidy.

As soon as the ball cracked Ty's bat, the PTA crowd stood as one, certain it was gone. The ball sailed over the outfielder's head and continued over the fence that encircled the field. Ty ran the bases in an easy jogging pace. When he crossed home plate a deluge of high fives from his teammates congratulated him.

"That was amazing." Cassidy hugged him, the best high-five yet.

"You haven't seen anything." Ty gazed at his buddies. "It's time to get the Bama boys back together when we take the field."

He called Mickey over to tell him his plan for defense positions: Dryden on the mound, Hunter first base, Bubba third and Ty replacing the high schooler as catcher.

The next batter struck out and the Bama boys took the field with their PTA teammates.

"Like old times." Hunter fired the ball to Dryden. "Let's go."

Dryden walked the first teacher probably because she looked terrified at the plate. They made an easy double play at the next up at bat. Two outs, the PTA ahead by one run.

One more out, game over. Bob managed to hit a single.

"Open your eyes!" Bob yelled at the next batter after he didn't swing at two strikes.

Ty called time out and went to the mound. "Throw high."

Before Dryden's pitch, Ty casually rubbed his hand on his leg signaling Hunter. The next pitch was a perfect lob. As soon as it hit his glove, Ty whipped the ball to Hunter who picked off Bob at first base when he slid back from his lead. Game over.

Bob faced off with Hunter spitting nails and questioning the call.

Hunter shut him down fast. "Act like a gentleman." He offered his hand.

Bob, apparently with effort, swallowed further argument and shook Hunter's hand. The dugouts and bleachers emptied on to the field.

Ty had a bead on Cassidy. He opened his arms, and she ran into them. Ty lifted her off the ground and twirled her around.

"Put me down. I'm getting dizzy." She giggled.

He set her on her feet. She gazed up at him, an

invitation in her sparkling green eyes. Ty bent his head slowly. His lips met hers. The noise of the milling crowd muted. There was only Cassidy. Her lips were soft and tasted sweet. He was lost.

Her eyes were closed when he ended the kiss, and she was breathing hard.

She opened her eyes and whispered, "Did you ever dream a kiss would be like this?"

"Every night, princess, every night." He ignored the people around them and he kissed her again.

Chapter 11

"Get a *room*," a bass voice, belonging undoubtedly to one of Ty's buddies, boomed.

Cassidy's cheeks burned as she broke the lip lock. Ty apparently had no intention of letting loose his possessive, strong-armed grip around her waist. Not that she minded.

She was tempted to stay put, but propriety won out, and she swiftly extricated herself from his warm embrace taking up a position by his side.

What was she doing making a display of herself in front of her small-town neighbors? Ty was already the favorite subject of the rumor mill. Cass suspected that the merry widow and the hot softball star would make chatty headlines the rest of that weekend. A weekend when she'd appear around town on Saturday night on an official date to add to the gossip. Cass thrilled at the prospect despite probably setting tongues wagging.

She looked forward to lingering longer in his company after the game that evening at the Cardinal Bar for a few victory beers and pizza, too. She was confident enough after his swoony kisses that he'd accept her invitation. He did. The Bama Boys horned in on the pizza party, too. Why not? They had played a huge role in the victory.

The parking lot emptied, and the softball teams' cavalcade of cars proceeded downtown for the fifteen-minute ride from the field. Winners and losers were up for the camaraderie. And probably starving for pizza. Donations to fund the lunch program had soared beyond expectations and Joelle was delighted. She was also more than curious about Ty's open PDA.

"So…" Joelle steered out of the lot behind Ty's truck. "You and sexy Ty Martin, huh?"

"Um…he's a good guy. Very kind. And a talented artist."

She hooted. "I'm sure he is. But you left out the smoking hot smooches in front of God and creation. I thought we'd have to call the volunteer fire department to save Memorial Field."

Cassidy rolled her eyes. "I was really embarrassed."

"Oh, get real. I'll bet you were so into that make out session that you didn't even know your own name."

She grinned. "That, too. Seriously, I really like him, Joelle. We're going out on a date tomorrow night."

Joelle brushed a hand on Cassidy's arm. "I'm happy for you, Cass. I have a good feeling about him."

"Thanks. Me, too. I've been so lonely."

"I know, honey. I know."

Finding a parking space near the restaurant proved challenging. Half the town converged on the Cardinal Bar and Grill. Johnny the bartender would work like a whirlwind that night. But Cass had thought ahead. Foresight had her setting out cones in two spaces fronting the bookstore after she had locked up for that night. The F-150 slipped behind Joelle's ex-husband's Mercedes into the second space while a stream of cars on Park Avenue trawled for non-existent parking. Ty and his friends met Cassidy and Joelle on the sidewalk.

The crowd that overtook the modest restaurant

formed a boisterous, shoulder to shoulder mob scene inside. Johnny, smiling all the while, slid mugs and pitchers of sloshing draft beer down along the bar to grasping hands. Pizzas were delivered to tables and perches at the bar with little fanfare and gobbled down with less.

Despite loving Ty's pulse ratcheting nearness, since he had no choice but to practically attach to her side, Cass became itchy for open space. Just when the edges of her vision blurred and a swimmy-headed faint threatened, Ty uttered her saving grace. "It's insane in here. Want to get some air?"

"Yes, please." *Definitely need air.*

Ty leaned sideways along the bar and nabbed a couple slices of pizza. He folded one in half, handed it to Cassidy and elevated his slice straight-armed above the crowd's jostle.

"Hold on to my belt," Ty directed. He turned toward the door and inched forward while Cassidy clung to the band of leather around his waist.

The evening still hadn't cooled but the rush of air that washed over Cass as Ty burst through the bar's door revived her.

"Thanks," she said. "I was starting to feel smothered in there."

"Much nicer to be alone with you," he said. "Are you sure you're all right? Want to find a bench and sit for a while?"

"I'm good. Maybe a little wrung out. It's been a long day."

"Let's stroll and finish this pizza. Then we can call it a night."

Blinking fireflies burst in tiny starry lights along the

walkway. Cass ambled by his side. She nibbled occasionally on the pizza in her right hand and dreamily clung to Ty's electric, warm hold on her left hand. Approaching her storefront where he had parked his truck, she marveled at the fates that had brought Sawyer and Ty into her life there. When she was with Ty, sorrow receded, possibility tantalized her and every nerve ending sizzled with desire.

He finished the last bite of pizza, slipped his hand into his pocket and pulled out a key fob. A shrill beep sounded and the locks on the truck disengaged with a pop. Ty pocketed the key.

"Can I give you a lift home? I'll come back and pick up the guys."

"Oh…" Cass gazed down the empty sidewalk towards the bar. "Since I came with Joelle I should see if she's ready to leave."

Ty grinned at her. "I get the sense that Dryden might be occupying her time right about now."

"Yeah. I think you may be right. I'll send her a text."

Cass pulled out her phone as Ty opened the passenger door on the truck for her. She climbed into the seat, sent the text and latched her seat belt. The truck engine roared and Ty steered out of the space.

The ten-minute ride home while they laughed and relived game highlights was way too short for her. Ty pulled up the long, tree lined gravel driveway leading to Cassidy's house and then braked.

Should I invite him in? She rejected the idea thinking it too soon to be that vulnerable to his charms in her private space. "Thank you for the ride. And most of all for playing in the game. It was amazing to beat the teachers."

"No problem. I had fun. Especially besting big balls."

Cassidy burst out laughing. "Yes. That was a highlight for everyone on the team."

"Let me walk you to your door."

"No need, Ty." She leaned over the console and pressed a soft kiss on his cheek, his beard stubble scratchy against her lips. "Oh…about tomorrow night. Can you please pick me up at the store at closing? We're open until seven on Saturdays."

"Of course. I have 7:30 reservations at *Sublime* on Serenity Lake. A half hour travel time at that hour should be perfect."

Cassidy lit up at his plan. "*Sublime*? Oh, Ty, I've wanted to go there forever."

She opened the car door, grabbed the handhold bar, climbed out of the truck and turned to face him. "Thanks again. Goodnight, Ty."

"Sweet dreams, sweetheart."

Warmed by his tender words, Cassidy floated along the path to her front door.

****

Another bolt of lightning sizzled a blazing spear through the charcoal-colored clouds followed by a resounding thunder boom that quaked the timbers of the bookstore. The lights flickered again which had Cassidy's stomach clenching with anxiety. She had less than an hour before Ty was due to pick her up for their dinner date. Trouble shooting a power outage wasn't on her agenda.

But Mother Nature had other ideas. The next lightning crack hit a transformer on the Park Avenue pole nearby. A shower of sparks visible through her front window preceded a total blackout. She used her cell phone flashlight to cut through the darkness and stared at her blank computer screen in dismay.

"Come on generator," she urged.

As if obedient, the generator kicked in and powered up the lights. Relieved, she rebooted her computer. Nothing happened. She unplugged the device, counted out ten seconds and plugged it in again. Nothing.

"Oh, come on!" She admonished the inanimate device while dialing Brian Cole's number.

Her tech guru picked up on the second ring. "Did the storm zap your database?"

"Yep. And I have to leave in forty-five minutes. Do you think it's possible to fix this by then?"

"What's the system doing? Are you getting an error message?"

"No, a completely blank screen. I tried to reboot, and I disconnected from power and tried again. The generator is running so I do have power. Hopefully they can fix the transformer on the block tonight. I saw lightning strike the pole."

"If you can't get the system to power up, I can't get into it remotely. I'll have to come to the store but at the earliest I can get there may be around nine PM."

"Okay. Thanks, Brian. I'll see you later."

She disconnected the call, calculating how to have her date with Ty and fix her integral database before tomorrow's opening, too. With a 7:30 reservation a half hour drive away they'd have less than an hour to eat dinner. Not exactly what she had in mind when she had gotten ready that morning. She had chosen to wear a sleeveless black dress with a cardigan and flats for work and then had changed into a sparkly shrug and strappy high heeled sandals for that evening. The *entire* evening, not a grab-a-bite and run out on him.

Cass called Ty to let him know about her problem, and thinking it best, to ask to postpone their date. He understood, said he'd change their dinner reservation to the following Saturday and asked if there was anything he could do to help.

She gratefully declined, glad that her budding relationship with him hadn't ended before it began. Then she drifted into the back office to do some paperwork while she waited for Brian Cole. She wasn't really hungry, but if that changed there was some food in the fridge.

Slogging painstakingly through manual business tasks that took too long to finish had Cass fully appreciating technology. She raised her head at the sound of the front door bell jingling. Checking her watch she rose to greet Brian. He had arrived much earlier than predicted.

"Cassidy? It's me," came Ty's distinct baritone.

Delight surged through her and she quickened her steps out to the front of the store. The sight of him took her breath away. His hair, made inkier by the downpour, curled at his ears and collar and the probably once crisp dress shirt he wore stuck to his chest in patches. Sexy, muscle framing patches. He obviously hadn't used an umbrella since his arms were full of a giant bouquet of scarlet roses, a champagne bottle and a shopping bag.

She scurried over to him accepting the flowers that he held out to her with a heart melting grin.

"Thank you, Ty. Roses are my favorite. They're gorgeous." Cass buried her nose in a velvety blossom.

"Just like you."

The compliment had her heart melting. It seemed everything Ty did or said had that effect on her. "Ooh. And champagne, too. What's in the bag?"

"Dinner, glasses for the champagne and some candles. I wasn't sure if you had electricity or not."

"*Really?* Oh, Ty, this is just perfect."

"Can't get to *Sublime* tonight, so I brought *Sublime* to you. Chateaubriand for two. Sound good?"

"It sounds amazing. Hmm. I think I have a vase in the back room."

"You go take care of putting the roses in water and I'll set out dinner for us."

When she returned toting the vase of two dozen roses, the room was candlelit. Ty had set the signing table in the alcove with dinner for two. He pulled out a chair and locked his magnetic gaze into her eyes. Drawn to him, her heart raced wildly, and she couldn't tear her gaze away from his sparkling blue eyes. She was entranced. As if floating, she set the vase down on one end of the table and gracefully sat on the chair. He smoothly moved her chair into position closer to her place setting and kissed the crown of her head. His breath and nearness both warmed her and sent shivers up her spine.

Shrill backup beeps sounded. Cass craned her neck and observed a cherry picker utility truck maneuvering into position beneath the transformer.

"Oh good." She unfolded a paper napkin and swept it over her lap. "Maybe we'll have full power back soon."

Cass turned her attention to Ty, his head bent over the champagne bottle. *So handsome.*

He popped the cork expertly catching fizzy overflow in a plastic champagne flute. He filled that flute and then another before handing one to Cass.

Cassidy raised her glass. "Should we toast?"

"Absolutely. To us and our beginnings here," he said.

"To our beginnings," She touched her flute to his.

Cass took a sip, set her flute down on the table and then gazed across the table at her beaming dinner date. Her focus was drawn over Ty's shoulder by a shimmery silhouette.

Sawyer?

The opaque, blurry outline of a figure suspended behind Ty for a few breathless moments and then disappeared like scattered sun motes.

She blinked rapidly and wagged her head.

"Are you okay?" Ty reached across the table and grabbed hold of her hands.

"Uh…yes. I'm good." Cass released her right hand and took a hefty gulp of champagne.

"You sure? You looked stunned there for a minute."

Like I saw a ghost.

"No really. I'm good. Everything looks delicious. Honestly, Ty. This is perfect."

"Great. I wanted our first date to be perfect, and I wasn't willing to wait a week." Ty withdrew his handhold and cut into the steak.

"I'm so glad you didn't." She sampled the chateaubriand. "Wow. *Sublime* lives up to expectations."

The entire evening surpassed her expectations except for its prim ending. Her tech had arrived shortly after she and Ty had finished their meals. He was discreet when he realized he had interrupted a romantic interlude, but he was still striding between her back room and her front checkout desk to fix her computer problems when Ty was ready to leave.

Cass had only a warm hug and a soft kiss on the lips to savor at the end of their first date.

Chapter 12

Ty burrowed his head into his pillow, smiling. Cassidy nestled against his shoulder, her soft hair tickling his cheek. He wanted to wake up every morning with her in bed next to him. How could he do anything but smile?

"I found her with Uncle Ty, Daddy," came a high pitched, far from soft whisper.

His eyes flew open. Harper stood next to his bed with her arms outstretched towards the famous kitten called Frances who lodged snuggly beneath Ty's chin.

"Daddy said we can't bother Uncle Ty, Frances." Harper's high-volume whispering had the opposite effect.

"Too late, princess, I'm wide awake." He tugged the sheets up to his neck over his bare chest. Frances pressed her soft body tighter into the crook of Ty's neck.

"Come here you little rascal." Harper jumped onto the bed and scooped up the kitten.

She stroked Frances's fluffy white fur grinning at her uncle.

Kane's tall figure filled the doorframe. "Sorry to disturb you at this hour, Ty. I thought we'd come early to start setting up for the BBQ."

"No problem. I don't want to sleep in today anyway."

Except to keep dreaming that Cassidy is in bed with

me.

"I appreciate the help," Ty said. "Let me take a quick shower and maybe drink a gallon of coffee and I'll be good to go."

"Sure. Come on, Harper."

He waited until they left the room before he threw off the covers because he never slept in pajamas. Ty headed to his en suite bathroom naked.

A beehive of activity swirled around him when Ty strode into the kitchen a half hour later. Maggie handed him an oversized mug of coffee.

"Bless you." He kissed her cheek and took a huge sip of the caffeine laden brew.

"You're welcome." She went to the sink where she washed fresh peaches, plums, strawberries and apples, methodically cut them into bite sized chunks, and filled large plastic bowls assembling the best of summer fruit salads adding in cantaloupe, honeydew, pineapple and watermelon.

Ty nabbed a strawberry out of a bowl and Maggie slapped his hand. He popped it into his mouth anyway.

"The butcher just delivered the meat." She rolled her eyes admonishing him for his pilfering.

"Kane put it in the coolers. Your mother said the caterers should be here…" Maggie glanced over her shoulder at the kitchen clock on the wall. "In about a half hour."

"Which means the tsunami known as mom should be here any minute."

The doorbell chimed.

"Right on time," Ty quipped.

Maggie wiped her hands on a paper towel and walked with Ty to the front of the house.

He swung open the door and his parents, Kamille and Brian blew past him toting huge trays of cookies. No Martin family get together was complete without an ample supply of Kamille's Kookies. Maggie and Ty trailed behind Mom and Dad into the kitchen.

Mom set her platter down on the countertop, turned to her daughter-in-law and gave her a warm hug. "Maggie you look radiant."

She trained her gaze on Ty narrowing her eyes. "You look skinny. Are you eating enough?"

"Good to see you too, Mom." He kissed her cheek.

Dad gave a head tilt toward the front of the house. "Come outside and give me a hand, Ty? The boys followed us. They're bringing the tables and chairs."

"Sure." Ty went outside with his dad.

Two power pickup trucks pulled into the driveway. His twin brothers, Jimmy and Martin and two pretty women exited the trucks with a crescendo of door bangs. The twins introduced their dates, Greta and Stacy, and then the group brought tables and chairs around the side of the house to set up in the back yard.

The sprawling lawn off Ty's deck seemed to shrink in size with the addition of two large grills and enough tables and seating to accommodate everyone. Chaos prevailed. The best kind. His nieces Harper and Meadow ran wild. Frances frolicked behind the little girls getting into the game.

Ty stood and observed his riotous family. Jimmy and Martin, with their girlfriends, set up the badminton net. Kane and Maggie positioned the corn hole board on the lawn. His sister Mary and her husband Marc laid out the beanbags for play next to the board.

He suddenly felt the odd man out. *Why didn't I invite*

Cassidy to the barbecue?

Jimmy and Martin argued loudly over a game of corn hole.

"The gang is starting to get hangry." Kane chuckled.

"On it." Ty fired up the grills.

****

Cassidy had decided to close the store at noon that Sunday. Park Avenue was a ghost town all morning. And she was exhausted after a fretful night. In her dreams she had kissed Ty who had turned into Sawyer and then back again. She didn't want to attempt to analyze that.

Cass relished a rare afternoon off on a perfect summer's day. She put on her favorite black and white polka dot swimsuit and a lacy, white crocheted cover-up. Charlie followed her outside and jumped up onto one of a pair of chaise lounges getting stuck halfway up to the seat. Cass placed a book, a glass of wine and a bone for Charlie on a cocktail table between the chairs and then put her hand under Charlie's rump to boost him up onto the lounger.

She settled into her chaise, took a sip of wine and let out a contented sigh. Glancing toward her dog in the neighboring chair, she giggled. Charlie lay sprawled on his back with his tummy fully exposed, tongue lolling, already sound asleep. Cass snapped a photo of him with her phone and then reclined her chair back and closed her eyes to sunbathe. The warmth of the sun and the soft breeze lulled her to sleep.

The sun had dipped lower in the western sky when Cass awoke from her nap and her sleeping pup no longer slept. His lounge chair was empty. She jumped to her feet, her heart pounding in her chest.

Cupping her mouth with her hands she yelled, "Charlie! Home Charlie!"

Cassidy stepped onto the lake's perimeter path, Charlie's familiar stomping ground.

"Hey, Honey!" Her next-door neighbor waved at her. "I saw him go past here a few minutes ago."

"Oh, thank you, Mrs. Jarvis. Down this way?" Cass pointed to her left along the path.

"Uh huh. I smell a BBQ. Knowing that little imp, my guess is he's headed toward grilled meat."

Cassidy huffed a laugh. "I'll bet you're right. Thanks again."

She broke into a jog along the lake's edge occasionally calling out Charlie's name. The smoky, savory smell of summer barbeque grew stronger. She saw smoke through the trees and the odor of burning charcoal intensified as she passed house after house.

Cassidy entered a clearing. Charlie sat next to a huge grill, adoring eyes trained upward on Ty and the tall blonde woman standing at his side. A stunning blonde woman.

Such an attractive couple.

The woman leaned close to Ty and said something that made him burst out laughing. Bitter jealousy speared Cassidy's heart.

His yellow T-shirt, tucked into yellow striped shorts, gripped his biceps and stretched taut against his broad chest and flat stomach. The scene in Ty's yard resembled a photo shoot for Ralph Lauren's summer line. Handsome men and beautiful women dressed in crisp, Lauren-worthy clothes played badminton, tossed beanbags into corn holes, gathered in pairs or groups laughing and talking and seemingly hung on Ty's every word standing by the grill.

Cass tugged on the hem of her short cover-up and snapped her fingers quietly trying to snag Charlie's attention before anyone noticed her.

Too late or too loud snapping. Ty looked up and caught sight of her. The smile that lit his face melted her heart. He put down the spatula he was using to flip burgers and ran down the slope of the yard toward her, turning his back on the blonde.

He wrapped his arms around her and kissed the crown of her head. "Just a few minutes ago, I was thinking of you and wishing I had invited you to my BBQ last night. How did you find me?"

He smelled of smoke and citrus. Cassidy could happily remain snuggled up against his chest. But gazing over his shoulder, she noticed that his guests stood mute and gaping at her.

Her cheeks flamed and she pulled away from him. "I didn't mean to crash your party."

She snapped her fingers again and glared at her errant dog. "Come on Charlie. Time to go home."

"This big guy is yours?"

"He is. And a shameless beggar. I'm sorry to disturb you."

"Sorry? I couldn't be happier." He clasped her hand and before she could resist, led her up the grassy incline into his yard.

"Everyone, this is Cassidy. Cassidy, meet my family."

Cassidy gave a slight wave of her hand. "Hi. Nice to meet you all."

Kane bounded over to her and Ty with a pixie-like pregnant woman in tow. "Maggie, this is Cassidy. She owns Cozy Nook Books."

"Oh my gosh." Maggie gave her a belly-bumping hug. "Thank you so much for being understanding about the book signing."

"No problem. It all worked out perfectly. Ty did you proud. Plus, your book is wonderful."

"You are too kind. You know Frances is here today."

Maggie scanned the yard and called Harper over. Cass petted the tiny ball of fluff in the little girl's arms while Charlie glared—if a Basset Hound could glare—at his mistress's paying attention to a cat.

A couple more introductions welcoming her into the fold ended with Cass holding a margarita in one hand and Ty possessively holding her other hand tightly.

"Come talk to me while I work the grill?" Ty said.

She gladly agreed.

"There is a steak with your name on it, buddy." Ty petted Charlie's head.

"Hey, Ty. I like my burgers mooing, okay?" came a female voice.

"Sure." He beckoned to the woman with his spatula. "Come over here a sec."

"Cass, this is Greta. She's with my brother Jimmy, the big guy over there arguing with the other big guy, my other brother Martin."

"Nice to meet you." Greta extended her hand.

Cassidy shook Greta's hand. "Nice to meet you, too."

"Greta just released a cookbook. Maybe you have it in your store." Ty took a burger off the grill, plated it and handed it to Greta.

"I write under the name G. Sweeny."

"G. Sweeny. Of course. I do carry your book. And, it's open on my kitchen counter right now to the recipe for your pepperoni pasta salad. I plan to make it tonight. I've had to reorder the book three times already. I can't keep it in stock. Congratulations."

"You're too kind. By the way, that salad is on the table." Greta pointed to one of the picnic tables loaded with food. "It's one of my favorites. Now you can try it and see if you like it before you make it."

"Maybe Greta can do a book signing in your store," Ty added.

"No." Greta spit out the retort frowning. "I would be too nervous. I better go and mediate Jimmy and Martin before there is blood." She hurried away.

"That was odd," Ty said.

"Not really. Not everyone can be a book signing star like you," Cass said. "I should take Charlie home so you can get back to your party."

"You can't leave. You haven't eaten yet and you have to try Greta's salad."

How could she resist that killer smile?

"I want you to stay. You belong here with me." He dipped his head and brushed a gentle kiss on her lips. "Please."

"I smell something burning and it better not be my steak," Kane yelled.

"Keep your shirt on, big brother." Ty finished cooking with Cassidy at his side.

He filled two plates and led her to the table where his parents and his sister, Mary and brother-in-law Marc were seated. Charlie trundled along with them and sat under the table at Ty's feet.

Martin and Jimmy bickered at the next table.

Although handsome and also identical to each other, they looked so different than Ty and Kane. They resembled their fair-skinned, red haired mother. Ty and Kane got their good looks from their father. Brian was extremely handsome, tall and muscular, with jet black hair and just a hint of gray at the temples. Ty's sister Mary had waist length nearly white, blonde hair and pale blue eyes—the stunning blonde that had left Cass bitten with jealousy earlier. Mary didn't resemble anyone in her family.

Ty's welcoming mom insisted that Cassidy call her and Ty's dad by their first names. Kamille had fiery auburn hair, porcelain skin and a ripping sense of humor. She launched into the story that had everyone laughing about Brian's insistence on naming their future children after she had named Hurrikane and Typhoon. He had picked the names James and Michael in the delivery room for the second set of twins.

"Wait." Cassidy looked at Ty. "I thought you said your brothers' names were Jimmy and Martin. Where is Michael?"

Kamille's face animated with glee. "When the nurse came in with the boys' birth certificates in the hospital, I thought she was verifying our last name and asked me to confirm baby Martin. I said yes. The nurse even asked again, and I repeated baby Martin. Well… apparently she was talking about first names… That's how our Martin Martin was named."

Her laughter was contagious.

Cassidy couldn't remember the last time she had laughed with abandon.

Stuffed and groaning, everyone pitched in to clear the tables and bring out a collection of desserts.

Jimmy passed around a plate of his latest creation:

chocolate brownie macadamia cookies. "I'd love your opinions, guys. I'm thinking about adding these to our special Christmas menu."

Cassidy took a bite of the delectable cookie. "Wow. I love it. I'd definitely buy them for the holidays."

"Oh, yes, Jimmy. I agree," Stacy said.

The verdict among the family was unanimous.

Jimmy flashed a wide smile. "Thanks, everyone."

Cassidy carried the last dish into the kitchen where Ty loaded the dishwasher.

Through the screen door she heard Kamille hollering. "Come on everyone. Thurston is here."

A collective groan arose from all quarters. Cassidy arched her eyebrows. "Who's Thurston?"

"You don't want to know. Come on." Ty took Cassidy's hand and led her back outside.

Kamille stood next to one of the picnic tables. Two large cardboard boxes sat atop the table.

"Thurston is my mom's assistant," Ty muttered in her ear. "Undoubtedly, he's here to take the dreaded annual family Christmas card picture."

"I think that's awesome."

"Yeah well. Stick around. Awesome isn't exactly how I'd describe this torture."

Kamille and Thurston unloaded wrapped packages from the boxes calling out individual names. Each Martin family member shuffled their feet retrieving their "gifts." Greta and Stacy seemed surprised when their names were called.

"Cassidy!" Kamille said.

"Huh?" Cass did a double take.

Ty barked a laugh and gave Cassidy a gentle nudge forward.

"Still think it's awesome?" he teased when she returned to stand at his side.

Cass looked down at the package she had accepted from Kamille. "How could my name be on this? No one, including me, knew that I would even be here today."

"My mom's a bit…"

Kamille clapped her hands. "Okay, off with you. You have fifteen minutes starting now. Thurston has to get back to Chicago. Ty, you can manage steering everybody somewhere inside where they can change."

Apparently, when Kamille spoke, the family jumped. Everyone returned to the yard in less than fifteen minutes wearing the matching Christmas pajamas that were wrapped in their individual packages.

Cassidy loved the green and white plaid, flannel pants and red long sleeve shirt with a reindeer's head that she had donned. Martin Family Christmas and the year were embroidered in the center of the shirt.

Thurston lined everyone up in rows. Cassidy stood in front of Ty flabbergasted that Kamille in ordering personalized shirts had not only known that she'd crash Ty's party but also, had known her size. The pajamas fit perfectly.

Martin Family Christmas. Kamille is including me in her family?

Thurston stood behind the camera's tripod. "On three everyone." He held up his left hand using his fingers for the countdown.

Charlie photo bombed the shoot in the last second plopping down on Ty's foot.

Amazed at Charlie's adoring connection to Ty, Cassidy quipped, "Do you have a hot dog in your pocket or something?"

"No," Jimmy said. "Ty's just happy to see you."

The entire group erupted in raucous laughter just as Thurston snapped the next photo. He took a lot more pictures, but everyone knew which one Kamille would pick for the card that year.

Chapter 13

"Don't you dare!" Cassidy extended her arms out in front of her with her palms up to ward off Ty's soapy sponge attack.

But he maneuvered around her defense first feinting left, then right, to land bubbles on the tip of her nose.

She used the dish towel to swab away the wetness. "I'm not going to dry any more dishes if you keep this up, Mister Martin."

"Ooh…*Mister* Martin. You're in the doghouse now, little brother," Kane said.

Charlie erupted in barking, maybe catching his cue from the word doghouse?

"Hush, mister," Cass commanded Charlie.

That drew a hoot from Jimmy. Or was he Martin? "She calls her dog mister, Ty. Now you know where you stand."

She bit back a laugh. "Well…I'm *very* fond of my dog."

Ty grinned at her and continued washing dishes. Cassidy picked up a barbecue spatula, dried it vigorously and then handed it to Kane to put away. Through the windows at the rear of the house, Cass watched pajama clad Martins, and honorary Martins, Greta and Stacy dismantling the picnic grove and hauling chairs and tables out of Ty's yard. Kamille stood on the fringe of the activity commandeering the operation.

Maggie drifted into the kitchen looking so cute in her maternity Christmas jammies. She arched her neck and gazed into her husband's eyes. "Harper and Frances are in the car. Probably fast asleep by now. I'm kind of tired, Kane. Are you ready to leave?"

"Go, go," Ty said. "We're just about done cleaning up. Drive safe."

Kane clapped Ty on the back. "I'd like to get home before dark. See you soon. Thanks for a good time."

He gazed at Cassidy. "Great to see you again, Cass."

"You, too, Kane. And lovely to finally meet you, Maggie."

Maggie gave Cassidy a warm hug. "I hope we can get together real soon."

The couple exited through the back sliding door trailed by a younger twin, presumably to say goodbye to the family in the yard, leaving Cassidy and Ty alone finishing KP. He pulled the stopper in the sink, the water drained with a sucking sound and then Ty used the spray nozzle to rinse away suds.

Cass dried the last bowl. "Where does this go?"

"Lower cabinet on your right. Bottom of the stack."

She stowed the dish and then straightened up facing Ty. "I should get Charlie home."

Ty glanced at the basset hound, sprawled on the mat in front of the sliding door in a food coma. "I think he's set for now," he said.

Cass giggled and then trained her gaze through the sliders at the back yard. "Looks like your family is ready to leave."

"Yep. Let's go say goodbye."

He clasped her hand and drew her out onto the deck, down the stairs and into the milling throng. Hugs were doled out and pleasantries exchanged. Cassidy and Ty brought up the rear of the parade around the side of the house to see everyone off in their respective cars.

Cass hugged Kamille last. "Missus Martin…I mean Kamille, thank you so much for today. I don't know if you know, but I'm an only child and my mom and dad have passed away—my mom recently. Being included as an honorary member of your family means a lot to me."

Kamille brought her hand to rest lightly on Cass's cheek. "I didn't know about your parents. I'm so sorry for your losses, Cassidy. But you are *not* an honorary member of the Martin clan. You are and will always be a full-fledged member of my family. My son is crazy about you. A mother knows."

Ty's mom zipped into the car leaving Cassidy speechless and gaping at her retreating figure through the windshield as Brian reversed out of the driveway.

Cassidy turned to Ty needing answers. "How did your mother know my name, my size and that I'd wander after my dog into your family party today?"

****

Ty debated how much, if anything to divulge about his mother's gift and those of her identical triplet sisters and the multiple generations of the *Sisters of the Legend.* He had never revealed family secrets to anyone. Not the Bama Boys or Melanie or any other girlfriends in the past.

Although he knew in his heart that Cassidy was different and entirely trustworthy, he didn't want to color their budding relationship by expecting her to wrap her head around the fantastical reality of his family's magical, extraordinary powers.

"I guess Kane told her all about you. And I'll bet Harper, too," he deflected.

"O…kay. Right down to the size clothes I wear?"

"Well, sure. Maybe in general terms. My mom's good with buying clothes for people. I'd really like to show you the house before you leave. I'm pretty sure Charlie is content."

It wasn't entirely a diversion. Ty wanted to enfold Cassidy in his world, and yes, confide in her his family secrets and answer any questions honestly—eventually.

Cass narrowed her eyes. "I'd like that, but I'm still confused. How did your mother know that I would be here today?"

Ty linked his arm through hers, securing her hand around his bicep. "I'm sure I mentioned to Kane that I was going to invite you. I had every intention to, but with the storm last night and your tech working at the store while we were together, I forgot to extend the invitation. Worked out great, though. I'm glad you could meet everyone. Come on." He tugged her into a stroll at his side.

"Want to see my etchings?" He waggled his eyebrows.

She beamed at him, her jade eyes dancing. "You honestly have etchings?"

"No. But it's a good line."

Cass chuckled. "Actually, it's a terrible line. But I'd love to see your art."

"Good. I'll show you my studio and get your opinion on some of the final decorating touches in some of the other rooms."

Back inside the kitchen, they stepped over snoozing

Charlie, and Ty ushered her to the front of the house. A two-story foyer leading to a flight of stairs separated the formal dining room and an office with built-in bookshelves. Like the true bibliophile she was, Cassidy was instantly drawn to his library.

The Chicago based interior designer he had hired to manage furniture selection and décor had stocked the shelves with leather bound classics. Ty explained that he had added his own TBR selections, a few mainstream fiction authors favored by his siblings and children's classics to entertain his nieces when they visited.

Cassidy perused the shelves like the pro that she was. She slipped one of the new releases off a shelf. "You like Harlan Coban?"

"Yep. I don't get much time to enjoy a good read, but he's high on my list of favorite authors."

"Me, too. Do you like the Reacher series?"

"Childs is another favorite of mine. How about you?"

"Love your favorites and I have a bunch more. You know…" she shot him a grin. "I'll give you a family discount at the store anytime."

Ty returned her smile. "That's very nice, thank you."

She re-shelved the book and turned to face him. "Can I peek at the dining room?"

"Of course."

Ty followed her across the foyer and stood beneath the arched entry to the room while she drifted around the mahogany table for twelve taking in the coveted seascape paintings he had hung on the walls.

"Yours?" she said.

He wagged his head. "No. Two are my cousin

Skye's works, and one is my aunt Karol's—my mom's identical sister."

"They're beautiful. You have a lot of talent in your family. And apparently a lot of identical twins."

"Actually, my mother, Aunt Karol and Skye's mom, Aunt Kay are identical triplets."

"Fiery redheads like your mom and younger brothers. Wow."

"Plenty of fire in my family for sure. Want to see the second floor?"

She nodded and then paced over to Ty meeting him at the dining room archway. He slipped his arm around her waist and led her to the stairway. Taking the stairs up to the bedrooms floor of his house while he kept his hand lightly on the small of her back, Ty imagined climbing his stairs with her every night to sleep in his bed. Even then on a simple guided tour, he knew in his heart she belonged there with him. In every family photo, every celebration, every quiet night in each other's arms.

Cassidy didn't think he needed to change any décor in the four bedroom suites that Ty showed her, deeming the wall colors and bedding and art in each room perfect. She complimented everything and was especially delighted when he brought her up another flight of stairs into his penthouse art studio.

She gasped. "Oh my gosh, the view is incredible!"

A half-smile curled on his lips watching her take in the natural beauty of the setting sun and crimson sky over Redbird Lake through his window wall. He stood back and let her wander among his paintings. He had crated and sent off most of the pieces slated for his showing in Chicago. A few completed canvases leaned on the walls on either side of the room. The last canvas he wanted to finish in time for the showing propped on an easel in the center of the bank of windows.

She studied each painting without saying a word making Ty suddenly insecure. No art critic's opinion was as important to him as hers. Cassidy finished her leisurely viewing in front of his work in progress standing transfixed by the painting of ten brilliant male cardinals interspersed on a background of pine green boughs.

"I am awed by your talent, Ty. This…this painting is beyond gorgeous."

He let out a breath he hadn't realized that he held making a mental note to exclude the painting from the show. It belonged to her. "Thanks, Cass. Your opinion means a lot to me."

Facing him, her face alight with a radiant smile and with the setting sun behind her casting a rosy glow around her enticing body in the demure one-piece bathing suit, Cass had never looked more beautiful. As if hypnotized, they slowly walked toward each other, and he drew her into his arms hugging her close.

"Come with me to my showing in Chicago next weekend," he proposed. "My events hosted by LM Galleries are usually really nice. I think you'd enjoy the evening. And you know as well as I do that the city is foodie heaven. We could have a candlelit dinner date in a real restaurant."

She arched her neck and gazed up into his eyes, an amused expression on her face. "You don't count our bookstore candlelit dinner as *real*?"

"It was great. But I want to wine and dine you in my favorite city in the country."

"I don't know, Ty…" A shadow darkened her jade

eyes. "Maybe we're moving too fast. I…"

"I'll reserve separate hotel rooms for us, Cass. I will never rush you or pressure you in any way. I'd just love to be with you and show you the town."

She gave him a soft kiss on the lips. He wanted to seize on the connection and deepen the kiss, but he held back respecting whatever boundary lines that she drew. "Can I think about it and let you know tomorrow?"

"Of course. It's starting to get dark. I'll walk you home."

"I'd like that."

Downstairs in the kitchen, Ty put together a doggy bag of leftovers for Charlie who awakened at the smell of steak and burgers nearby.

Cass petted the dog from the crown of his head along the length of his back making Charlie's hind quarters waggle. "Come on, Charlie. Home."

The obedient runaway slipped outside as soon as Cassidy slid the patio door open. Ty and Cass followed the dog arm in arm along the Lake path.

"Today was so lovely," she said. "Thank you so much for including me."

"If you're up for it, there will be plenty more opportunities. My city dwelling family is in love with my lake house. They don't hesitate to invite themselves."

She laughed. "I'd love to see them all again."

They walked in companionable silence in the soft air with the buzz-like drone of cicadas, bullfrog croaks and cricket chirps sounding in their ears.

Cassidy's sweet voice broke through the night creatures' chorus. "When would we leave for the showing?"

Her pronoun choice captured Ty's instant attention.

"On Friday morning. You said, 'we.' Are you interested in coming?"

"Yes. I think so. But I'm not sure I could leave on Friday. If Rina will cover the store Saturday and Sunday I could meet you in Chicago Saturday morning."

"Great. Whatever works best for you."

"I'll let you know for sure sometime tomorrow when I have the chance to talk with Rina. This is me." She pointed to a pristine three-story house on a hill off the path.

"May I have a good night kiss?" he said.

Cass answered by initiating a lip-lock herself. His blood heated in her sweet thrall. When she separated from him all he could think of was running his hands along the softness of her long legs and slim arms ravishing her on the spot.

She touched her hand to his cheek. "Thank you again for today. I still don't know how your mother knew everything."

"I've learned over the years that she is never wrong."

"Really? That's *very* interesting."

"Yeah. Why?"

"Because another thing that she told me was that you're crazy about me and I'll always be a full-fledged member of the Martin family.

"Nite, Ty." She hiked up the incline toward her rear deck.

Chapter 14

"Really, Cass? It's ninety degrees today and you think wearing a green velvet suit tomorrow night is a good idea?" Joelle said.

"But…" The outfit was one of Cassidy's favorites.

Joelle waved her hand in dismissal. "Nope. Check your closet for something for a fancy evening affair."

Rina and Joelle sat on the bed, sipping wine and rejecting every outfit that Cassidy modeled for them. They had proposed the girls' night to help Cass choose the perfect dress to wear to Ty's gallery showing the following night.

"You look like a nun," Rina said.

Cassidy did an about face without uttering a word. She crossed her arms and tugged the nun-like black, long sleeve, high necked dress over her head.

"I need a drink." Cassidy emerged from her bedroom closet in her underwear.

She hopped onto the bed with her girlfriends. The trio scooted up, leaned against the upholstered headboard and topped off their wine glasses from the bottle of Cabernet Sauvignon that Rina passed around.

"I thought it was a simple art show. I went to tons of them with Sawyer and I never had to worry about what I wore. Thank God Maggie called me this morning to let me know it was formal. She figured Ty didn't mention that. Typical male, he didn't. Maybe I should cancel."

"Over my dead body." Joelle wiggled off the bed. "I know you have dressier clothes. Where are you hiding them?"

"I'm not hiding anything…wait. Maybe I do have more clothes. After I sold the condo and moved in here, I think I put some dresses in my mother's closet."

"I'll be right back." Joelle scurried through the door out into the hallway.

Cassidy took a long drink of her wine. Tears welled in her eyes. "Thank you for coming, Rina. I don't know what I would ever do without you and Joelle."

"Oh, honey. We will always be here for you." She hugged Cass and then grabbed a tissue out of the box on the end table and handed it to her.

Cass cried at random for no reason. Her emotions were a chaotic jumble. In her dreams, she still wrestled with wanting both Ty and Sawyer with her whole heart. "Maybe it's too soon for me to start dating again?" She dabbed her eyes with the tissue.

"Only you can answer that question, sweetie. But I saw your face light up when Ty walked on to Memorial field to play softball. I saw your face after he kissed you. Sawyer is gone. Your marriage was filled with love until the day he died. But it's over now. Three years, ten years or twenty years—only you can decide. But one day you'll realize that your marriage to Sawyer is in your past and you'll want to move on. If you're asking my advice, I don't think it's too soon for you to start dating."

Joelle burst into the room waving a garment bag. "I found it. This dress is perfect. And it still has the tags on it."

"Let's see." Cassidy slipped off the bed and opened her arms accepting the garment bag from Joelle. "I'll be right back."

In her closet, Cass unzipped the bag. Happy memories came when she recognized it. She slipped on the silky dress and sashayed out of her closet.

"Yes!" Joelle and Rina chorused.

The midnight blue, sleeveless sheath fit Cassidy perfectly. The silky material skimmed her body, from the mandarin collar to the high slit up to her thigh.

"You look killer sexy," Rina said. She scooched off the bed.

"Thanks, honey. I kind of feel sexy in it. I forgot all about this dress. I bought it when I was on a shoot with Sawyer in Thailand. Sawyer was diagnosed right after we came back to the States from the trip. We didn't go out anymore."

"You should wear your hair up in a bun, and I would go with only simple jewelry." Rina opened the lid of Cassidy's jewelry box which sat atop her dresser and picked out a pair of earrings.

"These are perfect. Simple and elegant." She displayed her choice in the outstretched palm of her hand—white gold studs in the shape of roses.

"I love those earrings. They were my mom's. Dad gave them to her on their last Christmas together. She couldn't believe that he bought her something from Cartier. I think the box is still on the shelf in her closet."

Cass picked the earrings out of Rina's hand, paced over to her dresser and inserted the studs gazing at her reflection. She twisted her hair up and fastened the bun with a couple bobby pins.

Joelle emerged from her closet dangling a silver shoe in each hand. "I think these shoes are killer. Try them with the dress, Cass."

She stepped into the four-inch-high heels and struck a pose for her friends. "I feel like a princess."

"You look like one, too." Joelle said.

Rina nodded agreement and then the pair converged on Cass and drew her into a group hug. The evenings' work dressing Cassidy concluded, and the girls' night continued gobbling down pizza, watching a Hallmark channel movie and falling asleep together on the king-sized bed.

****

Cassidy started out at ten thirty in the morning and made the trip downtown the next day in less than two hours finding the traffic light on rural routes and highways. It was a familiar drive that she had made almost weekly visiting her mom after Sawyer died. She felt liberated from her daily business worries and responsibilities with Joelle and Rina managing the bookstore and Joelle's dog-sitting Charlie overnights at Cassidy's house.

The Waze app provided directions along Wacker Drive to the Monarch Hotel where Ty had booked rooms for them. The cityscape unfolding on the riverfront brought a wide smile. Cass loved Chicago in all its colors. The Chicago River wound under spans of bridges as busy as any thoroughfare with tourist boats and pleasure boats sailing toward and away from Lake Michigan. Pedestrians jammed the sidewalks, a diverse milling throng of people enjoying the summer day.

She steered into the circular drive fronting the hotel, braked at the valet stand and popped her trunk. A bellman whipped her small suitcase and garment bag out of the back of the car and then opened Cassidy's door for her. She left the car, deposited the keys in the valet's hand and followed the bellman through the revolving doors into the softly lit lobby.

While the front desk clerk finished the check-in process, Cassidy texted Ty to let him know that she had arrived at the hotel. He still hadn't texted back when she pushed the "up" button at the elevator bank. With her envelope containing her plastic room key in hand, she stepped inside the car, swiped her key over the wall pad and depressed the button for the twenty-first floor.

Nervous that the momentous weekend away with a man other than Sawyer was truly beginning, she checked her reflection in the mirrored walls of the elevator. Cass tucked the sleeveless white blouse into the A-line black and white polka dot skirt that she wore for something to do with her shaking hands.

The pneumatic doors swished open. She gasped in delight, earlier nerves forgotten, at the sight of Ty standing directly in front of her and gifting her with his radiant smile. He wore a crisp white linen shirt tucked in to black, form-fitting jeans and held out one delicate long-stemmed red rose to her.

She stepped out of the car and accepted the fragrant flower from him. "Thank you, Ty. This is lovely."

"I'm glad you're here." He kissed her lips briefly making her stomach clench and leaving her wanting more.

Ty clasped her hand and led her down the long hallway, their footsteps muffled by the plush carpeting. He pushed open a door at the furthest end of the hall that rested unlocked on the dead bolt arm and then propped open the door leaning his back against it.

"I reserved a two-bedroom suite. I thought you could still have your privacy and also we can enjoy the living room and dining room together without having to go out into the hallway. But…" he continued rapidly. "I'll change to separate rooms if you're at all uncomfortable."

"No need, Ty. This sounds perfect."

"Great. We have a kick ass view."

Cass swept past him into the room and Ty let the door shut behind him with a click.

"Oh my…" She blinked her eyes scarcely believing the beauty before her.

Yes, they had a spectacular view seemingly suspended in the midst of skyscrapers with the panorama of the Chicago River below. But the view inside the room was even more spectacular.

Vases of roses were placed all around the living room and in the center of the dining room table for six—an explosion of aromatic sweetness and pastel and vibrant hues.

"You mentioned roses are your favorite, but I had no idea which color. So, I ordered a dozen of each color the florist had."

"This has to be the most extravagant thing anyone has ever done for me." She blinked away tears. "Wow, Ty. Thank you so much."

"I didn't want to make you cry. I was shooting more for you'd run into my arms and kiss me." He grinned.

So appealing. So generous. So irresistible.

On a laugh, she flew into his arms and kissed him. He fused his mouth to hers, heating her blood and stoking escalating need. She threaded her fingers in his soft hair as he tightened his arms around her, and she melted into the embrace molding her body to his.

To her chagrin, Cassidy's stomach veritably

howled. She froze and felt his grin stretch against her mouth.

Mortified, Cass drew away from him, a flaming blush creeping up her neck to the roots of her hair. "I'm so embarrassed. I meant to eat breakfast, but I got distracted and wanted to get on the road as early as possible. I think I have some nuts here in my tote bag."

She slipped the bag handle down from her shoulder and peered inside.

"No need for snacks, Cass. I was starving and I ordered a couple of club sandwiches from room service. Should be here any minute."

"That's amazing. You've thought of everything. Thank you."

A loud bell chime sounded.

"Whoa. We have a doorbell and everything?"

"Why yes. I believe we do," Ty tossed over his shoulder in motion toward the door.

The bellman and the room service steward had arrived at the same time. Ty took her suitcase and garment bag in hand and paid a tip to the bellman.

"Please come in," Ty directed the steward.

"Shall I set the table for you, sir?"

"Yes, please," Ty said. "Cass, I'll put your luggage in your suite. Be right back."

Ty held the door open for the room service attendant pushing the empty cart and then closed it behind him. "Alone at last…"

The doorbell sounded again.

"Hold that thought." He answered the door.

A young man handed two pizza boxes and a plastic bag to Ty and accepted the ten-dollar tip. The door closed again.

"My goodness. Just how hungry are you, Ty?"

"I was in the mood for pizza but didn't know if you liked pizza or not. I ordered the club sandwiches just in case."

"You're kidding, right? How could I live in Chicago and not like pizza?"

He set the two boxes from different pizzerias down on the dining table and emptied the plastic bag containing paper plates, napkins and utensils. "Ah, but here is the big deal breaker. Gino's or Malnati's?"

She picked up a plate, opened the box of choice, and plated a wedge of rich, cheesy, gooey, deep-dish pizza after she took a huge bite.

"Malnati's," Cass said with her mouth full.

"I found my soulmate," he said on a laugh.

Ty helped himself to two slices of Lou Malnati's deep dish pie and took his plate over to the couch positioned before the wall of windows that afforded the kick ass view shimmering in the sunlight.

Cassidy helped clean up the paper plates and napkins after they had stuffed themselves with pizza— the untouched club sandwiches wrapped in napkins and stowed in the mini-fridge.

Ty checked the time. "I thought we could do some sightseeing but it's getting a bit late to be back here in time to change for the show. Are you okay with just staying here? We could have a glass of wine and watch the world go by."

"That sounds perfect." She kicked off her shoes and sat on the couch tucking her legs under her.

Ty uncorked the wine and brought the bottle and two glasses over to the coffee table in front of the sofa. He poured their drinks, sat next to her, and draped his arm around her back massaging her shoulder in slow circles. His warm touch sent thrills through her.

"This is such a gorgeous view." Cassidy snuggled closer to him.

"It certainly is." Reflected in the glass, Ty looked at her instead of out the window.

She tilted her head up to meet his penetrating gaze. Slowly he inched closer, and his lips met hers. He trailed kisses on her cheek and along the side of her neck triggering waves of sensual jolts in her core reawakening long dormant desire. Cass kissed him deeply while she slowly undid the buttons on his shirt.

His stomach muscles clenched as she tugged the shirt out of his pants and trailed her own line of kisses from his neck to his belt and back up again to his mouth. He cupped her face with his warm hands letting loose a deep-throated groan.

An alarm blared splitting them apart as if scalded.

"You have got to be freaking kidding me." He tore the watch off his wrist and threw it across the room.

The discordant alarm just kept blasting sending Ty on the chase to find his watch on the floor.

She clapped a hand over her mouth. Her shoulders shook with her muffled giggling.

"Are you laughing at me?" He looked up at her from the floor on all fours.

That made her laugh harder.

"This afternoon has *not* gone as I'd hoped." Ty rose to his feet, the alarm silenced at last.

She got off the couch and gave him a hug. "It has been perfect. I wouldn't change a thing.

"Did you set the alarm for when we have to dress for the evening?"

"I did."

"I better get started." She brushed a kiss on his lips and paced into her suite.

A vase filled with multi-colored roses graced one of two bedside tables. The man was very good at wowing her.

Cassidy considered an opulent soak in the jacuzzi tub but decided to leave that for when she had time to spare. The quick hot shower with forceful water pressure felt opulent, too. She blow dried her hair haphazardly without styling and then pinned the updo leaving a few loose tendrils framing her face. After taking pains applying her makeup, she donned her dress and put on her jewelry.

She opened her bedroom door and took a couple of steps into the living room. Ty leaned against a window frame gazing out at the vista. His shower-damp hair curled around his ears. He wore a tux with the top button open on his starched white shirt. An untied bowtie hung around his neck. What was it about a man in a tuxedo? Pure heart-pounding seduction.

He turned and faced her. His gaze traveled the length of her body and then he walked towards her.

Her breath caught at the expression in his eyes—fiery, intense desire.

"Wow." He drew her into his arms and kissed her softly. "There are no words to describe how beautiful you look."

"Oh, Ty…"

He silenced her by fusing his mouth to hers.

She didn't want the dizzying, sizzling connection to end and would happily forego the evening out to stay alone with him in a romantic cocoon.

But that night was a big deal to Ty. She wasn't surprised when he ended the kiss and said, "We better leave before it's impossible for me stop kissing you."

Cass gave him a half smile and linked her hand in his thinking in that moment that she would follow Ty anywhere.

Chapter 15

If Ty didn't sell a single painting that night he would still consider the evening an unprecedented success with Cassidy on his arm. Walking down Illinois Avenue with her beside him, enjoying the light breeze off the lake, he felt blessed with good fortune. He ushered her into LM Galleries, named for its proximity to Lake Michigan rather than after the owner, Larry Melrose, as most people assumed. Ty thought about sharing that bit of trivia about the initials on the discreet gallery signage with Cassidy, but Jessie sped over to them and he knew better than to compete with the gallery's energetic curator for conversational airtime.

"Hi Jess…"

The slim, statuesque redhead clad in a figure flattering, sleeveless black dress went in for a hug and gushed, "Ty, you've outdone yourself this time." She squeezed most of the air out of him. "Honestly, I wanted to hide half the paintings in the back, save my money and scoop them up for myself."

She moved on to continue her hug fest with Cassidy whose eyebrows shot up in Jessie's clutches. "Hello, it's so good to see you," Jess said.

"Cass, Jessie is the gallery's curator and the owner's daughter."

"Yes. Hi, Jessie," Cassidy squeaked out.

Jessie unhanded his lady and took a backward step

smiling widely.

"Jess, this is Cassidy Finnegan…"

"Oh, I know, I know."

Ty knit his brow. "You know?"

Cass touched his arm. "We've met several times before, Ty. Sawyer's work was shown here."

"True, true." Jessie clasped her hands at her waist. "Ty, can you please tour the gallery and let me know if everything is up to your expectations?"

"I'm sure that's not necessary. You always do exceptional work and…"

"Humor me. May I bring you some champagne? Wine? Water? The caterer is almost done setting up the hors d'oeuvres table in the solarium and I can offer you something more substantial. Let me know if anything's off with lighting, pricing, etc., Ty. Just because things were to your liking before, doesn't mean that I've gotten it right this time. You decide where and how you want your work displayed. And of course, if you want any price adjusted up. Never down. But you already know that. Shoo, shoo…" Jessie waved them into motion.

The curator spun on her heel and zipped away leaving Ty bullet ridden, as usual, by her verbal machine gunning. He smiled down at Cass. "I guess I better do what I'm told. Care to join me?"

"Of course." She chuckled. "Sawyer never did a thing that she told him to do. Drove her crazy."

Ty halted in his tracks. "Wait. You mean I won't be punished if I don't toe the line?"

"Oh, you'll be punished all right. My advice is don't go there."

"Noted." He huffed a laugh and glanced at his watch. "We have about ten minutes before the show opens. Let's walk the circuit, even though I already know that I'm not changing anything."

He drifted from canvas to canvas appreciating Jessie's eye rather than finding room for criticism. Unlike some gallery showings where display lighting was one-note, each work was individually lit depending on the mood, medium, and color palette of the work: pale yellow, soft amber, dim white and dramatic florescent. He never found fault with Jessie's display instincts nor questioned her pricing. His commissions from each successive show there were increasingly impressive.

Ty held Cassidy's hand and breezed by each painting moving through the pre-show drill. He was jittery for the first time since he was a newbie gallery artist. In so many ways, he was his work. Cassidy's opinion of his artistry seemed inseparable from how she regarded him in general.

He wouldn't fish for compliments nor compete with her husband's reputation, but he would be happy if she thought his talent at least up to par.

She exceeded his humble expectations. "You are amazing. If I were rich, I'd buy every single painting before anyone walked through that door. I can't wait to study each work."

"Thank you, Cass. I'm so glad you like my stuff." He brought the back of her hand to his lips and kissed her satiny skin.

Before Ty could inspect the hangings in the annex, the gallery door swung open with a whoosh. Ty's family flooded inside led by take-charge Kamille. Ty and Cassidy were assaulted by the multi-hug fest and love fest that was the Martin family.

"Ooh, I can't wait to go shopping," Kamille said.

"Ma, you know you don't have to pay for my paintings. You never make me pay for your cookies."

"No comparison. Come on, Brian. Let's check out the exhibit."

Ty wagged his head. "There's no stopping her no matter what I say. At least Jessie knows that where my family is concerned, I forego commissions."

He turned his attention to the front door. Jessie had materialized from the back of the gallery where the solarium was located. She took up a post in front of the door next to a small glass table wearing a broad smile and an Italian designer black suit jacket over her dress, ready to supply customers with the catalog of the evening's offerings.

Uniform clad, white-gloved servers toted trays of champagne flutes and offered morsels to eat: mini-quiches, lobster rolls, shrimp, bacon wrapped dates and Ty's favorite bite-sized pigs in a blanket.

Soft piano music played through hidden speakers: instrumentals of Kane's compositions. Jessie was adept at personalizing her artists' showings.

Ty delighted in squiring Cass around his familiar territory introducing her to patrons he had met before and meeting strangers with her whom he hoped might appreciate his work. She seemed to enjoy the scene bestowing radiant smiles to every person that she encountered.

Jessie left a stack of catalogs on the glass table by the door when the influx of prospective customers lightened. She expertly chatted up folks lingering in front of pieces. Ty knew from experience that she would gauge serious interest and then call him over to help clinch the sale.

The gallery door opened and two brawny men wearing earpieces and telltale bulges under black suit jackets lumbered inside and headed to Jessie. She conferred with the men while murmurs arose from the customers around Ty and Cassidy.

"What's going on?" she said.

"The Mayor's here. That's her security detail."

"No kidding? You know the Mayor?"

"Let's say she can put my name to my face because she's a fan. Want to meet her?"

"Sure. Will those big guys frisk me first?"

Ty hooted. "No one lays a hand on my lady. Come on. There she is."

****

Cassidy's admiration for Ty grew as the obviously successful event wore on. Society notables, VIP's and art critics counted among the sizable crowd. And it seemed that these people weren't there to simply browse and gobble hors d'oeuvres. They were serious art lovers who kept Jessie hopping and affixing sold signs beneath paintings.

Ty was reluctant to leave her side, but she shooed him away frequently to tend to customer demand assuring him that she was having a great time and she wanted him to feel free to do business. She strolled lazily around the perimeter of the gallery eavesdropping on conversations and stopping to gaze at his works that caught her eye.

She had completed a half circuit when she found herself next to Ty and a pretty sandy blonde woman. The woman gazed longingly at a painting of Wrigley Field at night. A white flag with a blue W waved in the upper left corner of the canvas. The illuminated sign on the stadium read:

WRIGLEY FIELD * HOME OF CHICAGO CUBS * WORLD SERIES CHAMPIONS

"I was back home in Chicago that night watching the away game on TV at the Cubby Bear Bar. I moved to California from Chicago almost twenty years ago. Doesn't matter. I'm a lifetime Cubs, Bears, Bulls and Hawks fan. It was the most thrilling night in memory when my Cubbies beat the Indians and broke the curse. Everybody, including me, was dancing in the street. I really want to buy your painting, but I see a Sold sticker below it. I'm so disappointed."

"Hmm," Ty said.

"You know what?" He edged his thumbnail under the Sold sticker, removed it and stuffed it in his jacket pocket. "It's yours if you want it. I know the buyer and it won't be a problem."

"*Really?* Oh wow! I have the perfect place to hang it. Thank you *so* much. Truly, I'll cherish it."

"No problem. Let me get someone to help you." Ty waved a hand at Jessie.

And then he shook the woman's hand. "Thank you, miss…I'm sorry, you didn't mention your name."

She grinned at him. "It's Jen. Great to meet you. Do you think the gallery can ship to Oceanside, California?"

Jessie bustled over to them.

"Here's the lady to help you. I know they can ship anywhere in the U.S. Enjoy. Safe trip home." Ty stepped to Cassidy's side.

"Is the original buyer going to be angry that you resold that painting?" Cass said.

"Nah. I painted that for my dad's birthday gift. I have until November to duplicate it."

She could kiss the man. He always acted from a place of kindness and generosity. Gorgeous, sexy, sweet and kind. Cass marveled at the fate that brought them together.

"Are you the artist?" came a gruff voice.

Ty turned toward the man. "I am."

"I have a question for you."

"Go. I'll be fine," Cass urged Ty.

"You sure?"

"Absolutely. I haven't seen everything yet. And I can always go hang out with Maggie or your sister or mom. Don't worry about me."

"I'll try to make it quick. I'd rather hang out with you." He winked at her and walked over to the man with a question.

Cass floated from painting to painting stopping to gaze intently on each striking work of art. The realism that Ty achieved in his paintings was incredible. Even though he wielded a brush instead of a camera, Ty and Sawyer had a lot in common as artists. She lingered in front of the canvas dominated by vivid green pine boughs and roosting brilliant red cardinals that she had seen in Ty's studio. A soft smile curled on her lips at the Sold sign beneath the canvas. He had promised to give the painting to her. She widened her eyes reading the price tag.

Good grief, ten thousand dollars?

She'd have to find him before the showing was over to tell him to take the sold sign down. He shouldn't forego a lucrative sale like that.

"Hey, Cassidy. Find anything you want to buy?" Kane sidled up beside her.

"A little rich for my budget. How about you?"

"Yeah, I'm a sucker for my brother's art. Did you see the black and white painting of three little girls? Over there on the far left?"

"Yes. I think so."

"They're my little cousins. I bought it for their mom. She's my cousin, Skye and an artist herself. But she's going to go nuts over that painting."

"I agree. Ty's work is amazing."

"It is. I think Maggie and I are heading out."

"Did I hear my name?" Maggie lumbered over approaching that stage in pregnancy where she moved in a wobble. She appeared wan and bleary-eyed.

Kane took one look at his wife and circled a protective arm around her. "Come on, little mama. I think it's past your bedtime."

Cassidy hugged each of them in turn and wished them good night.

A waitress approached Cass and relieved her of her empty champagne flute. "Another glass of champagne, miss?"

"Why yes. Thank you." She took a delicious sip. Cassidy was no connoisseur, but she could tell that she drank the finest champagne.

"Cassidy, dear. Can I borrow you for a minute?" Kamille called out.

Despite having met the lady only once before, Cass recognized the motherly demand wrapped in a courteous request. She snapped to attention and hustled over to Ty's mother's side.

Kamille stood in front of two paintings cupping her chin with her hand. One was a dreamy watercolor of mist rising over water throwing a gauzy curtain over the surrounding shadowy forest. The other painting was striking in its starkness. A large expanse of lawn rendered in a green so dark it appeared black was home to a single, tiny cardinal—a miniscule pop of brilliant color.

"Which one should I buy, dear?"

Cassidy was powerfully drawn to both pieces. "Hmm. Do you know where you'd like to display the painting?"

Kamille chuckled. "You know I never do until I get the painting home or to my business headquarters."

"Well, what's the color scheme of your home and at work?"

"White walls everywhere. Minimalist, I guess you could say."

"They both perfectly fit in with that scheme. I wish I could be more help, but they're equally captivating. You can't go wrong with either one."

"Well, I guess it's decided then. I want both." Kamille turned around and faced her husband who hovered behind her. "Brian, can you please go find that young lady salesperson for me?"

She patted Cassidy's arm. "You have excellent taste. Thank you."

Chapter 16

Kamille conducted business with Jessie despite Ty's assertion that his mother didn't need to spend money on his art. Cassie moved to stand before the next painting.

"Cassidy! Hi." Ty's sister, Mary, her face glowing with a broad smile, bustled over to Cass.

"I'd hoped that you'd be here tonight." Mary's hug was quick and firm. "It's great to see you again."

"Great to see you too. I know Ty appreciates his family's support."

"I almost didn't make it in time. Traffic was terrible, so Marc dropped me off. He and Meadow headed straight to the hotel."

"You're staying in a hotel? I thought you lived in the city."

"No. We live in the burbs. Marc commutes into the city for work. We moved to the Western suburbs for the schools when Meadow was born. They're the best in the area. Oh, here is the man of the hour."

Ty sauntered over to them. He slipped his arm around Cassidy's waist and drew her close to his side warming her from head to toe.

"As usual you're late, sis," he teased. "Where's Marc?"

"He took Meadow to the hotel. You're still planning to take her home with you tomorrow, right?"

"Yes…of course."

"Good. Staying at Uncle Ty's is all that she's talked about all week. Oh—she wants to see Charlie again, too, Cassidy."

"We can make that happen, especially if Ty lights his BBQ again. I'm positive Charlie will find his way back to Ty's house," Cassidy said.

"What a great day that was. Wait until you see the Christmas card this year. Mom showed it to me. It's hysterical. Hard to believe, but before you know it the holidays will be here. I can't get my head around school starting up again so soon. I feel like the summer just started."

Mary glanced at the delicate, diamond watch on her slender wrist. "I better run. I have to say hello to the fam before I go. See you tomorrow morning. Let me know what drop off time works for you both." She breezed away from them after doling out two quick hugs.

Ty watched her hurry away. "Wow, she's exhausting," he quipped.

"You didn't remember that Meadow was coming home with you, did you?" Cassidy said.

"Nope, what gave me away?"

"I'd have to go with the blank stare." She snickered.

"Well, there goes my plan for a romantic breakfast in bed tomorrow morning." He winked at her.

She didn't know whether or not to take him seriously. Would she love a romantic breakfast in bed with Ty? Yes.

His brothers appeared out of the crowd taking up a position in front of Ty and Cass. "The team will do well this season. I think the rookie quarterback looks promising, right Ty?" Jimmy said.

Ty opened his mouth to respond, but Martin

interjected, "No way. The guy's too green."

Cassidy squeezed Ty's hand and left him to argue about the Bears chances with his brothers. She had yet to view the whole exhibit and enjoyed taking her time in front of each piece.

She watched a woman touch a canvas gently. "I can't believe I can feel brush strokes. Amazing, this looks so real," she remarked to the man at her side.

"I have to have it," the woman said.

The man immediately waved Jessie over to him and finalized the deal. Many of the paintings bore tiny red stickers, SOLD.

Jessie approached Cassidy. "Can I get you anything, another glass of champagne?"

"A pair of soft fuzzy slippers would be nice."

"Dogs barking?" Jessie grinned.

"Howling."

"I might have a pair of flats in the back. What size shoe do you wear?"

"Oh, don't bother. I was just kidding. I'm good. The showing seems to be going well. So many red stickers."

"I predict that we'll sell out before the end of the event."

Cassidy turned the corner into another section of the gallery and gasped at the first painting in line on the wall.

"Are you all right?" Jessie hurried to her side.

"I'm…fine."

"Excuse me, ma'am?" came a male voice.

Cassidy pointed out the man to Jessie. "That gentleman is trying to get your attention. I'll bet you have another sale."

Jessie frowned. "Are you sure you're okay, Cassidy? You look a little pale."

"I'm sure." Cass forced a thin smile. "Go help that customer and put another red sticker on a painting."

Cassidy couldn't catch her breath studying the painting on the wall in front of her. Sawyer had snapped that exact image of her on their honeymoon. In the painting, as in Sawyer's photo, she was depicted from behind gazing out a window while holding open a gauzy curtain with her right hand. She wore a sheer, white negligee with her blonde hair pinned up in a top knot, loose tendrils trailing down her neck and the sides of her face. The painting captured the photo in intricate detail down to the lace on her gown and the hint of her naked form through the opaque material.

The first night of their honeymoon was everything Cassidy thought it would be and more. The morning after, Cass had hopped out of bed awakening before her brand-new husband.

"What are you doing out of bed my love?" Sawyer's voice sounded gravelly from sleep. His tawny hair stuck up all over his head.

"I can't sleep. I'm too excited," she said still captivated by the scene outside. "I can't believe I can look out our hotel window and see the Eiffel Tower."

She heard the click of his camera and smiled. "Don't you have enough pictures of me?"

"I can never have enough pictures of you, my love. Come back to bed. It seems I can't sleep either."

He didn't need to ask her twice.

Sawyer had developed that photo in his darkroom and had only produced one wallet-sized print. It was his favorite picture of her which he had kept in his wallet. There was no way Ty or anyone else could ever have seen that picture. How could Ty possibly have painted her on her honeymoon? Why would he put something so private on display for the world to see?

How could this happen?

Did Sawyer somehow convey the image to Ty?

Impossible.

As much as she wanted to make excuses for Ty, she felt staggered, humiliated and ripped in two. Sawyer. Ty. Tears welled and she brushed them quickly away. She needed to leave.

She slipped out the gallery's side entrance, hopefully unseen, when the Uber she had ordered arrived. Seated in the backseat of the ride, Cassidy took her phone out of her purse to text Ty. She changed her mind and didn't compose a message to him, needing some time alone to wrap her head around the strange occurrence.

Cass desperately wanted to understand. But whatever Ty's explanation, she was too shaken to deal with it that moment. She slipped her phone back into her purse after using the App to tip the Uber driver, scurried into the hotel and headed straight for the elevator bank.

Tears threatened again when she was greeted with the fragrance of dozens of roses in the hotel room. She sagged down to a seat on the couch holding her head in her hands.

She needed to formulate a plan to sort things out. Looking around the beautiful suite with its unbelievable view where the memory of Ty's kisses lingered, she knew she couldn't stay there. Cass changed out of her formal clothes into leggings and a tunic top and packed her things.

Before calling the Bell Captain to bring around her car, she jotted a note to Ty on hotel stationery, brought it into the living room of the suite and propped it up against a vase of flowers on the credenza where he'd surely notice it.

Back in the bedroom to gather her belongings, her heart flip-flopped and her hands shook when her phone pinged a text notification since she was desperate to avoid engaging with Ty until her head cleared. Thankfully, the message was from Joelle.

—Charlie is with me at my house, Keith had something come up at work and had to drop the kids off. Hope you're having the BEST time.—

Attached was a picture of her boys cuddling with Charlie on Joelle's couch.

Her friend wouldn't expect her to answer that night. Best of all, Cassidy would return to an empty house with no need to explain her early departure from her romantic weekend away with Ty.

She touched the velvety petals of the roses in the vase on her bedside table. He was so thoughtful and kind. There had to be an innocent explanation for his intrusion into her honeymoon. But she couldn't face a possible confrontation with him in her state of confusion. She rolled her suitcase out of her bedroom and then stopped short at the door. Retracing her steps, she took the vase of flowers off her bedside table, dumped the water out in the bathroom sink and took the roses with her.

Driving away from the city, the illuminated skyscrapers receded in her rearview mirror and darkness cocooned her in the car. Her pounding headache lifted, convincing Cass that she had made the right decision to leave. She turned on the radio and listened to music, willing herself to stop thinking and just drive.

It was nearly midnight when she pulled into her

garage. She unloaded her trunk and brought her things into the house leaving her suitcase in the middle of the kitchen, too exhausted to unpack. Cass filled a vase with water, arranged the roses and set the flowers on her kitchen counter.

She trudged upstairs to her bedroom longing to sleep away the strange evening. Too tired to change into pajamas, she shimmied off her bra from under her shirt and plopped down on the edge of her bed, compelled to open the bottom drawer of her end table to sort through its special contents before she lay down.

Memories swamped her.

Six months after Sawyer died, her mom had made a surprise visit to her condo determined to have a serious talk with her daughter.

Honey, I know you're hurting but it's time for you to start living again. You don't want to hear this—I didn't either when Dad died. But, you need to clean out Sawyer's things. He's not coming back. I promise you that as hard as it is to accept this, you'll feel better when you do. When your Dad died, a day came when I knew I had to stop living as if he were coming back to me. I needed to give you back the mother you deserved. So, I cleaned out one drawer in my bedroom and I put all my favorite mementos that I had of my life with your dad that would fit in that drawer and then I let the rest of it go.

Cassidy had known that her mom was right, but it was terribly hard to put her advice into action. Her mom stayed with her throughout. After a week and a million tears, Cassidy had condensed her life with Sawyer into a drawer in her bedroom end table.

Her hand trembled as she took a few of the mementos out of her drawer. She smiled at the plastic

Oscar award for the best husband with Sawyer's name on it which she had given him during the last Academy Awards ceremony before he died. They had loved to watch the Oscars together snuggled in bed with junk food. There was a small stuffed pig that Sawyer won for her in a claw game at the diner on one of their first dates in the city and a photo booth picture from Navy Pier where they had both made crazy faces for the camera. She pushed things aside until she spied what she searched for at the bottom of the drawer—his worn, brown leather wallet. Hidden behind the drivers' license and credit card slots she found the small, laminated picture Sawyer had taken of her on their honeymoon. Just as she remembered it. Exactly how Ty had painted it. Tears streamed down her face as she carefully put everything back in the drawer.

Usually, she had Charlie to cuddle with when the world without Sawyer became too much to bear. That night she was totally alone.

She curled up on the bed, closed her eyes and sobbed into her pillow. Cass felt his strong arms around her pulling her close to his chest and spooning with her as he had done almost every night of marriage until he became too impaired by illness.

You are not alone, my love. I am always with you.

Was she dreaming? If so, she didn't want the lovely fantasy to end.

"Sawyer," she whispered, "I've missed you so much."

No answer. She hadn't expected one. She closed her eyes and drifted off to sleep.

Chapter 17

"You two." Ty clapped a hand on Jimmy's shoulder. "Do you ever agree on anything?"

Martin gave him a crooked grin. "Occasionally."

"Yeah," Jimmy piped up. "Like Go Bears. Go Cubs. Go Bulls. Go Hawks."

"Right. Just not the pregame and postgame analysis," Martin said.

His family had always united rooting for Chicago teams. But Martin and Jimmy fought fiercely over just about most things as adults and everything as kids. Mom had rarely attempted to referee even when they had punched the crap out of each other. Kane and Ty were docile in comparison.

"Where are Greta and Stacey? I figured since you introduced them to family you guys are serious?" Ty said.

The twins nodded in unison. "Stacey moved into my place a month ago," Jimmy said. "She has fallen in love with so many of the paintings tonight."

"Really, does she have a favorite?" Ty asked.

"She pointed out the one you did of the beach with the seagulls about ten times." Jimmy laughed while Ty made a mental note.

"Greta loves all the cardinal paintings," Martin added.

Ty added a cardinal painting to the Christmas list he

put together in his mind.

"Her mom always told her that cardinals were visitors from heaven. Good thing they all have sold stickers on them." He laughed. "She still lives in her own apartment. I'd love for her to move into my house, but she wants her space. Guess she's not ready to commit."

"Are you?" Ty asked.

"I think I am. But I am not going to rush her. She's worth waiting for."

"Yes she is," Jimmy chimed in. "We won't keep you from your adoring public."

"We're going to head out now. We drove together. I'm really proud of you, Ty." Martin hugged him.

"Me too," Jimmy gave Ty a hug and then followed Martin in search of their ladies.

Ty scanned the room, looking for Cassidy.

The throng of art lovers and would-be patrons had seemingly multiplied since he had started talking with the twins, but her beauty would stand out in any crowd. He didn't find her in the main gallery, so he headed to the annex.

Ty was waylaid several times on the way. With contrived patience, he answered questions and where interest was high, handed prospective customers off to Jessie. He rounded the corner and entered the annex where browsers were fewer, but Cassidy wasn't among them.

The Mayor breezed into Ty's orbit with burly bodyguards bookending her advance toward him clearing people in her path just by virtue of their scowls. The unstoppable, trim, petite blonde was used to the sea parting in front of her whether she shopped the art gallery, the stores at Water Tower Place or up and down

Michigan Avenue. She was notoriously stylish and an avid consumer of fine things. Considering that his originals were the only works of art gracing the walls of her home, Ty thought that the lady had great taste.

Despite his eagerness to find Cassidy, he had to pay undivided attention to one of his most loyal customers.

"Madam Mayor." He was tempted to kiss the back of her hand, but he knew any move to touch those two muscle-men's protectee would probably put him in a chokehold at the very least.

"Did you find anything you like this evening?" Ty said.

"Of course." A smile softened her features making her look less like she was itching for a fight—her usual demeanor. "You've always added touches of nature to even your cityscapes, but this collection is saturated with flora and fauna. Makes me want to go for a walk in the woods or take a boat ride on a secluded lake."

"I'm glad you like the exhibit."

She guffawed, her distinctive attention-grabbing laugh. "I must have. I bought four pieces. If my husband even had the slightest clue about the price tags, he'd kill me."

Ty grinned back at her. "Your secret is safe with me, your Honor. Thank you."

"No. Thank you. I love your work."

"Thank you again."

"Come on boys. I'm ready to leave. See you next time, Ty. And don't forget to vote in the next election."

"Of course. You always have my vote."

She nodded her head, sealing his vow. "Good night, Ty."

"Good night, ma'am."

One more area to search remained. Ty had only paced a few steps before a female couple blocked his path.

"Are you T. Binder?" one of the pair said.

"I am." He held out his hand for a shake.

The speaker accepted the handshake with a surprisingly forceful grip. "I'm Cindy," she said. "And this is my wife, Barbara."

"An honor to meet you," Barbara said. "You're extremely talented."

"Thank you very much. Can I answer any questions about a specific piece or the showing in general?"

"Yes. Do you ever donate paintings to charity?" Barbara said.

"I have."

"Would you be willing to donate a painting to an auction we're hosting?"

"Which charity will benefit from your auction?"

Barbara looked at Cindy and raised her eyebrow. Cindy nodded.

"It's a charity that touches our heart. Cindy beat breast cancer this year. We were staying at our summer home on Redbird Lake when she was diagnosed. Looking at your beautiful paintings we assume you know Redbird Lake."

"You're correct. I just built a house on the Lake, and I live there permanently now."

"Cindy had to go all the way to Chicago for her chemo treatments. We decided to raise money to add a cancer center to the hospital in Redbird to make it easier on patients who have to undergo the same treatments." Barbara squeezed Cindy's hand.

"We've organized a gala later this month here in

Chicago and we would love to have one of your paintings to auction," Cindy added.

"I'm honored to donate a painting." He took a business card and a pen out of his pocket, wrote his personal contact info on the back and then handed it to Barbara.

"This is my private email and phone number. Let's touch base the beginning of next week and we'll iron out the details. Oh…And please put me down for two tickets to the gala. It's a pleasure to meet you both. You're doing valuable work."

He shook their hands in parting. At last no one vied for his attention. Ty hustled toward the solarium in search of Cassidy. In his rush he almost missed the first painting on the wall of the annex—the gauzy, out of his customary wheelhouse, boudoir painting that was the first he had created in his Redbird home studio.

Ty pulled up short in front of the wall hanging and looked around for Jessie, waving her over when he spied her.

"Yes, Ty?" She caught her breath.

"How did this get here, Jess?"

She knit her brow. "I don't know what you mean. I love this painting. So unusual for you, but it's mesmerizing. I've had four inquiries about it tonight so far. The would-be buyers are still here making their final purchase decisions."

"Can you do me a favor right now?"

"Of course."

"Please take it down and wrap it for me? It's from my private collection. I never intended to sell it. The courier must have taken it by mistake."

"No problem. But are you sure? The price I've

quoted is very lucrative."

"I'm sure. Thank you, Jess."

He sped away toward the solarium leaving Jess to the task. Ty ducked his head into the room where the caterers had set out hors d'oeuvres. He encountered a few plate-toting folks drifting around the buffet table, but Cass wasn't there, either.

"Huh," he said under his breath.

He spun on his heel and returned to the annex.

Jessie raised her head and smiled at him when he entered the room. "You need something else, Ty?"

"Have you seen Cassidy?"

"Um…" She looked around the room. "Last time I saw her, she was in this room. Did you check the solarium?"

"I did and she's not there. Do you think maybe she's in the ladies' room?"

"Possibly. Actually, she looked a little pale. I hope she's not ill. I'll go check for you."

"Thanks."

Ty waited impatiently for Jessie to return concerned that she thought that Cassidy might feel sick. His anxiety magnified when Jess appeared wagging her head.

"She's not there, Ty."

"Thanks anyway. I'll go find my mom and dad. I'm sure they'll know where she is."

But his parents were clueless, too. Ty hustled to Jessie's office where he had left his cellphone for the duration of the event. It seemed to take forever to turn on. The wait was to no avail. She hadn't texted him.

He fired off a text to her.

—Hey, sweetheart where are you? Are you okay?—
Send. Delivered.

Tapping his foot, he stared at the screen hoping to see the bobbling three dots appear preceding her answer. He waited for five minutes. Still no answer. Rather than leave the phone in the office again as was his custom when working a showing, he silenced the ringer and slipped the device in the pocket of his tuxedo pants hoping that the phone would vibrate soon with her response.

The evening dragged on. Ty was so distracted with worry that he was thrown way off his game. He had to force amiable conversations with prospective customers and secretly grit his teeth before answering the same routine questions about his technique and media over and over again.

His parents were among the last to leave.

"You'll let us know when you hear from Cassidy?" Mom said.

"I will." Ty gave her a warm hug. "Thanks for coming."

"Always." She patted him on the cheek. "I'm so very proud of you."

Dad shook Ty's hand. "I agree with your mother, son."

"Means a lot, Dad."

He watched his parents' retreat, tamping down a surge of envy. Ty wanted a love like theirs. He had thought he'd found it in Cassidy. How could she leave without saying a word to anyone? Surely, he hadn't misjudged her nature. Wasn't she too polite and caring to behave so coldly?

Ty itched for release from his professional obligations to go in search of her.

Finally, Jessie flickered the lights and shouted out

the announcement that the event would end in fifteen minutes. Ty shook a few hands as customers departed. When Jessie locked the gallery's front door, he made a beeline for Jessie's office.

He waited while Jessie wrapped the painting of the woman that somehow reminded him of Cassidy ready to flee the second that she finished.

"Want me to wrap the other one of the cardinals for you?"

"No, thanks. You can ship that to me."

"Great." She handed him the painting.

"Thanks for your hard work tonight, Jessie. You did an amazing job."

"My pleasure, as always. Dad will be thrilled with tonight's receipts. You better believe he'll want you back when you're ready with inventory."

"Deal. See you soon, Jess."

Outside in the mild night, Ty hailed a cab needing to get to the hotel as quickly as possible. When the driver braked in the hotel's circular driveway after the ten-minute ride, Ty handed him a twenty-dollar bill and bolted out of the car.

Traversing the lobby, waiting for the elevator and riding up to the twenty-first floor seemed to progress in slow motion. He swiped their room door open and bounded inside.

"Cass!" he called out. "Are you all right, sweetheart?"

Blinded by trepidation, he set the painting down on the dining table and rushed into her room. The adjoining bathroom door was ajar—empty. Her bedroom was empty, too, and her bed was still neatly made.

Unable to stop frowning, Ty drifted back into the

living room where he spied a handwritten note on the credenza. He raced over and snatched up the note.

Dear Ty, I hope you can forgive me for leaving your showing without a word. I was very upset and confused and couldn't stay. I do love you, Ty. But I realized tonight that I can't give you all that you deserve. I'm so sorry for running off and hope we can talk when you return to Redbird. Please don't contact me until then. Love, Cassie

Ty balled up the paper and tossed it in the trash can. Wandering over to the window he stared blankly out at the city's illumination while his mind reeled.

What did I do? Why was she upset and confused? How can she tell me she loves me, but it's not what I deserve? Shouldn't I be the judge of that? How did this all go sideways on me?

He slouched in a chair at a loss for answers. A myriad of emotions warred inside him: disappointment, disbelief, worry, frustration and, admittedly, anger. How could she tell him what he most wanted to hear and in the next sentence take it away? He didn't deserve more than Cassidy's love? What in the world did she mean?

Ty took out his phone ready to defy her wishes and dial her number. His lock screen displayed the time. Eleven PM. Would she be home already? On the road? More questions he couldn't answer since he had no idea when she had left the gallery.

He held the phone limply in his hand deciding to respect her wishes and delay contacting her until he was back in Redbird. Thinking about his return home, he remembered his promise to his niece.

Focusing on his phone screen, he opened the text APP and typed a message to Mary.

—Bring Meadow to the Monarch Hotel any time that's good for you in the AM. I'll be up early.—

He tossed his phone on the coffee table and continued to gaze out at the magnificent view in solitude that he had planned to share with the woman that he believed was the love of his life.

Chapter 18

Cassidy spent a quiet morning rising late and reading the Sunday paper while leisurely sipping her coffee. Since Rina didn't expect her at the store all day, she took a long bath and then decided to attend the noon Mass at St. Mary's Church. Heading out the door, Cassidy took the vase of roses that she had brought home from the hotel with her to put on the front counter of her store.

There was a bake sale after the Sunday service, so she stopped at the table to support the CYO basketball team.

"Cassidy, I was hoping I would see you today." One of her regular customers and a participant in her store's book club manned the table.

"Hi, Maureen. Everything looks delicious." Cassidy dug her wallet out of her purse.

"I wanted to talk to you. The Woman's Guild is thinking about starting a book club for inspirational Christian fiction. I was wondering if you could help us select some books to start us off."

"I would love to. I have a great selection of inspirational books at the store, and I have a few personal favorites that I could recommend."

"That would be great, thank you. I'll stop by the store this week." Maureen tried to give her change for her purchase, but Cassidy waved it away as an extra donation.

"I'll put a few books aside when I get to the store."

"Thanks a lot, Cassidy. See you soon."

She stowed the large box containing a dozen cookies and a dozen homemade donuts that she had bought on the back seat of her car. Just thinking about cookies brought vivid memories of Ty and his family. Cass closed her eyes and wagged her head a couple times trying to banish him from her jumbled thoughts. Impossible.

In the driver's seat, she sent a quick text to Rina to tell her she was on her way—back early because Ty was spending time with his niece for a couple of days returning them sooner to Redbird than originally planned.

Mickey's paint van was parked next to Rina's car in the bookstore's adjacent lot. Curious about why both of her friends were at work in her store, she unloaded the car and knocked on the back door with her elbow.

Rina answered her knocking and swung the door wide open. "Here, let me take that big box for you. Oh yum. I smell chocolate. I'm starving. What beautiful roses."

"Why is Mickey here?" Cassidy said.

"Come with me." Rina led her to the front of the store. "Surprise!" She pointed to a beautiful wooden bookcase with multi-sized shelves.

"Oh, my goodness. It's exactly as I envisioned it. Mickey is amazing. Where is he?"

"He just ran out to get coffee. Hold on a minute."

Rina deposited the bakery box on the alcove table and took her phone out of her pocket. "I'll text him. Would you like a tea with lemon?"

"That would hit the spot."

Cassidy put the vase of roses on her front counter and then drifted back over to admire her new piece of display furniture.

She ran her hand over the smooth polished surface of the wood. "The notecards and bookmarks are going to look amazing on these lower shelves and I love this large shelf on top. I thought each month I could feature a new book here. I have the perfect thing for this month."

She zipped into the back room and brought a package back out front.

"I just got this in." Cass unpacked a fluffy, white stuffed kitten from the box, placed it on the shelf and set a copy of the *A Kitten Called Frances* next to the stuffed animal.

"Wait until Mickey sees that. It looks great. He's worked on building this for you nights because he's been so busy at work."

The carpenter himself appeared out front toting a cardboard tray with three large cups. Cassidy hustled over to open the door for him.

"Thank you so much, Mickey." Cass relieved him of the tray.

"For what?" His powder blue eyes gleamed. He strode into the store, and she followed him over to the alcove.

Cass set the tray down on the table next to the bakery box. "It's exactly what I wanted Mickey. I can't thank you enough. How much do I owe you?"

"You don't owe me anything. It's a gift." He smiled. "But I would like one or maybe two of those doughnuts."

"Deal."

They sat around the table sipping their drinks and

feasting on pastry. Rina filled Cass in on the activity at the store while she was gone. She pointed to the rainbow roses on the front counter. "From Ty?"

"Yes. Would you believe when I walked into the hotel suite there were vases of different colored roses all over the room? He said he didn't know what color I liked so he bought a dozen of each."

"Oh, how romantic." Rina crossed her hands over her heart.

"Hey. I do romantic things, too." Mickey said. "Didn't I bring you a double cheese pizza last night?"

Rina snorted. "You sure did, honey. Good thing you were there to help me eat it."

Cassidy beamed a genuine smile at Rina and Mickey. They were just what she needed that day to help her get over the shock and improbability of Ty's painting Sawyer's intimate photo of her. She loved the Lynches so much. They were family.

After the drink cups were drained and a large dent was made in finishing off her bake sale bounty, Cass suggested, "Why don't you two leave and enjoy some Sunday relaxation? I'll close up. And then I have to run to Joelle's to pick up Charlie."

"Before we go there's something we want to tell you." Rina bit the corner of her lip and glanced at Mickey who gave her a nod.

Rina's apparent nervousness made Cassidy's stomach clench. *Please God don't let it be bad news.*

"Okay. Here goes." Rina took a deep breath. "We've decided to try IVF one more time. We start next week."

Tears welled in Cassidy's eyes. "That is the *best* news I have heard in a long time. I'm so happy for you."

"We're not going to tell many people, but we

wanted you to be the first."

"I'm honored and I won't tell anyone. Group hug!"

Cassidy walked with them to the back door. She was still smiling when Rina's car and Mickey's truck disappeared from view.

She selected *Jewel of the Adriatic,* one of her personal favorites in the inspirational romance genre, and a few other titles from the Christian inspirational section of the store for Maureen's new book club and put them by the register. No customers were likely to stop by that late Sunday afternoon in the quiet town, so she decided to lock up and go to Joelle's house to pick up Charlie.

Seated behind the wheel of her car, Cassidy texted her ETA to Joelle—ten minutes.

Charlie greeted Cassidy with full body wagging ecstasy when she walked into Joelle's home. The doorbell chimed a few minutes later.

"Dinner." Joelle opened the door and accepted the Chinese food delivery. "I called as soon as I got your text."

Joelle set the kitchen table for two, poured a couple glasses of wine and told Cass to dig in. She didn't hesitate. Somehow she was still hungry despite scarfing down a donut earlier.

"Where are the kids?" Cassidy said.

"Keith picked up the boys a little while ago. He felt bad that he had to bail this weekend. He's going to keep them overnight and then meet me at Wrigley Field tomorrow night for a Cubs game." She bit into a crab Rangoon and sighed.

"The boys must be so excited to go to the game." Cassidy helped herself to some fried rice.

'I'm pretty excited, too." Joelle wiped her mouth on a napkin. "I haven't had time to tell you, but I've been talking with Dryden."

"Ty's Dryden?" Cass stopped chewing.

"Do you know another Dryden?" Joelle chuckled. "Yes. Ty's Dryden."

"That's great. I thought I saw sparks between you two at our baseball game."

"So far we've just talked on the phone. For hours." Joelle had a dreamy gleam in her brown eyes. "He invited me to the game tomorrow night in his company's suite. I asked him what company he works for. He said Walker Communications."

"I've heard that's a really great company to work for." Cassidy put an egg roll on her plate.

"He said I can bring my boys, too. I asked if he had enough tickets so I could ask Keith and Travis. That's when he told me that by his company he meant *his* company. I had never asked his last name. It's Walker. He owns the company and the suite at Wrigley. Apparently he has a suite at the United Center for Hawks and Bulls games and everything. Wow, right?"

"I would say that is a big wow."

"We're all really excited. But enough about me. I'm dying to hear about your weekend. Start at the beginning and don't leave anything out." Joelle took a sip of her wine and sat back in her chair.

Cassidy began by telling her about the hotel and the dozens of different colored roses and all the food that Ty had ordered. A muffled text tone sounded. Cass rose from her seat and plucked her purse off the kitchen counter to retrieve her phone.

The message was from Ty: a photo of a sweet Basset

Hound puppy with the caption,

—*Meet Charlene.*—

"Oh, how adorable. Ty just sent me a picture of a Basset Hound puppy." She held the phone out to show Joelle the photo, but a series of notifications sounded vibrating in her hand.

He sent a photo of himself with Meadow and the puppy and another of a full PetSmart shopping cart.

The last text read:

—*Do you think my sister is going to kill me?*—

Cassidy burst out laughing. She handed the phone to Joelle to take a look.

Joelle grinned and handed the phone back to Cassidy who responded,

—*Well duh. Yes she will.*—

—*Oh well. At least I will die Meadow's favorite uncle.*—

came his response.

Cassidy read his last text to Joelle which brought on their fit of giggles. Cass dropped the cellphone on the table as her laughter turned to tears. She full-out sobbed.

Joelle widened her eyes, grabbed a handful of napkins and shoved them into Cassidy's hands. "Oh my God, Cass. What's wrong?"

She picked up Cass's phone and reread the texts. "What did I miss? Did Ty say something? Did I do something? Please, Cass, tell me why you're crying."

"I'm sorry. I don't know what came over me." Cassidy sagged in her chair and blew her nose in a napkin. "It's Ty, not you."

"What did he do to you? Was it something that happened this weekend?" She reached across the table and held Cass's hand.

"The weekend started out perfect, so romantic with all the roses…" She paused.

"Did you sleep with him?"

"No. Just a lot of delicious kissing before the show. However, if he had said let's blow off the show and stay in this hotel room and make crazy love all night, I would have in a minute. It felt so right, Joelle. All he had to do was ask and we would have shared a bed."

"But?"

"But we went to the show, and it started off great. His family was there, and they couldn't have been kinder. He was as attentive as he could be with all the customers wanting his attention. Then it happened."

"What happened?"

"He was busy with his brothers, so I looked around at all his amazing paintings by myself. One of his paintings was of me. I couldn't believe it. I think I went into shock."

"Why? Isn't that kind of a compliment?"

"I guess, normally. But this painting was *exactly* like the photo Sawyer took of me in our Paris hotel wearing a negligee the first morning of our honeymoon. I mean exactly."

"Could Ty have seen Sawyer's work?"

"Maybe, but not that photo. Sawyer loved that photo of me the most. He developed it in his darkroom and only made one small print that he kept in his wallet. No one other than Sawyer and I have ever seen it. Not even my mom. When I got home last night I even checked Sawyer's wallet to make sure it was still there. It was."

She closed her eyes for a moment remembering the warmth of Sawyer's arms around her in bed. Cass had never experienced that closeness with Ty. What would that be like?

"Did you ask Ty for an explanation?"

"No. I was in a state of disbelief. It's a tasteful portrait. You can't see my face and it isn't too revealing. But it's very intimate and private to me. Seeing it flooded me with beautiful memories of Sawyer. I panicked and had to leave. I called an Uber, left the gallery, packed up my stuff at the hotel, got in my car and drove home. I left a note for him in the room, but I didn't explain why I was so upset that I had to leave. I was confused and I felt like my heart was split in half. When he just texted, I guess it opened up the floodgates. I'm sorry for being dramatic."

"You don't have anything to be sorry about. There has to be an explanation for how Ty painted the picture. I can't believe that Ty would do anything to hurt or embarrass you. I've seen how he looks at you. I think you should give him a chance to explain."

"You're right. I want to. You always know how to make me feel better. I love you. Maybe I'll call him tomorrow, but right now, pass the sesame chicken. Crying always makes me hungry." Cass dug into the food determined to believe her friend's opinion that the weird occurrence had a logical explanation.

Chapter 19

Meadow's animated chatter during the car ride to Redbird slightly distracted Ty from constantly thinking and worrying about Cassidy. Only slightly. He had woken himself up talking in his sleep questioning her when he had finally nodded off in the chair the night before—or was it that morning? His head felt hangover-muddled even though he hadn't had a drop of alcohol at the showing.

Cassidy-obsessive thoughts kept breaking through the cotton in his head.

"Do you like that, too, Uncle Ty?"

"Uh…" He blinked a couple of times, but he couldn't formulate an answer. His niece's monologue leading up to the question was lost on him. "I'm sorry, Meadow. Like what?"

She giggled, a pretty tumble of bell tones. "Nana's new cookie cakes, silly. I want one for my birthday and Christmas and Daughters' Day."

Ty raised an eyebrow. "Daughters' Day? Is that really a thing?"

"Oh yes. It's in September and I'm really looking forward to it."

"I'll bet. So what? Is it like Mothers' Day with presents?"

"Oh no. Just a treat. Momma says gifts are only for her special day because she labored hard and long to bring me into the world."

Ty snorted a laugh. "Sounds like my sister."

He exited the highway and steered down the ramp to access the rural route that was a straight shot to Redbird Lake. Ty would avoid driving through the quaint Redbird downtown—entirely too masochistic a trip for that day.

"Nana says even though I'm her granddaughter and not her daughter, she can still honor me on Daughters' Day. And Momma likes it because she doesn't have to do anything."

Ty burst out laughing. "Now that *really* sounds like my sister." He was grateful for the little girl's company which unexpectedly helped lift his spirits.

Ty vowed to enjoy Meadow's visit and put aside love life problems even though he rankled at the strange limbo in which Cassidy had left him. "So do you think I could score one of those treats for my birthday?"

"Of course. Nana loves to feed the whole world."

That brought a smile to Ty's face. "That she does, sweetheart."

Driving through the outskirts of town Ty spied the PetSmart sign and turned into the parking lot on impulse.

"Why are we stopping here, Uncle Ty? Are you buying a toy for Frances or Tornado?"

"Better than that. Come with me, sweetheart. Time for a surprise."

Her face glowing, Meadow took his hand and walked into the store with him. A few leashed dogs, tails wagging, trotted in front of their owners in the aisles. Ty directed Meadow to the back of the store to view the puppies. Less than an hour later, the duo left the store: Ty toting a doggie bed, a couple of gates and a stuffed shopping bag of food and puppy supplies and Meadow carrying a wiggly female basset hound pup in her arms, wearing a wonderstruck expression and a Christmas came early smile.

When he entered his house peace descended upon him. The place held nothing but natural beauty and wonderful memories—the best of which was the Charlie invasion of his barbecue that brought Cassidy to his home and into his family. Maybe that's why he had become so fond of basset hounds that he had to bring another into his family. Indirectly. Without the ownership burden.

Mary is going to kill me.

Meadow was all smiles and energy, like a wiggly pup herself. She obediently leashed the puppy and took her outside to begin training. Ty set the dog's bed in the warmth of a pool of sunshine near the patio door and erected a couple of gates to restrict any accidents to the easier to clean kitchen floor area.

As soon as Meadow returned with her new best friend, the puppy curled up in her new bed and fell immediately to sleep.

"May I go to your studio, Uncle Ty? Harper told me about the painting of the three little esses that you made. I really want to see it."

"Three little esses? I don't know which one that is."

"You know…Serenity, Spring and Scarlet? Cousin Skye's babies?"

He snorted a laugh. "Right. I get it now. I'm sorry, sweetie. But Uncle Kane bought that painting last night. To give to your cousin, Skye."

"Oh, pooh. Harper said that she couldn't tell it was painted. It looked like a photo to her. I wanted to see if I can find your brush marks."

An elementary school art critic. Hopefully, he'd pass muster. "Well, sweetheart, there's plenty of other paintings up in the studio. Feel free to wander wherever you want. I'll fix us a couple sandwiches for lunch and then I'll be right up."

She pointed to her carry-on sized, roller suitcase. "Where should I unpack?"

"I'll bring that to your room when I come up."

Freed to roam, Meadow zoomed up the stairs. Ty paced into the kitchen, opened the fridge and hung over the door scanning the shelves. *Grilled cheese it is.*

A loaf of bread, a package of cheddar cheese slices and a tub of butter in hand, Ty pulled out his largest frying pan from the bottom drawer underneath his six-burner stove top and went to work fixing lunch. While the first side of the sandwiches sizzled in the pan, he checked his pantry for the perfect accompaniment. Tomato soup—a must with grilled cheese.

He opened the can, dumped the soup in a saucepan and set it to simmer. Wielding the spatula to turn the sandwiches he focused his thoughts solely on Meadow, determined to have fun with the little girl who had stolen his heart from the moment he had held her in Mary's hospital room.

After his mom, Ty was first in line to babysit Meadow whenever Mary needed a break or when her work schedule was full. Mary was the president of Kamille's Kookies and Mom occupied the office of CEO. His work hours were flexible and left ample room for watching kids' shows about heroic animals and piglets' families during the workdays with his tiny niece. While he had sat on the rug, Meadow had toddled around him, sometimes plopping down on the floor and using him as a human pillow-rest.

Ty had taught Meadow to swim in the rooftop pool of his condo building and had taken her countless times in her stroller to Navy Pier and Lincoln Park Zoo. When she was older, he broke the bank taking her to the doll extravaganza on Michigan Avenue. Who knew a doll needed a hair salon? She, to that day, had declared Ty her favorite uncle and he did nothing to discourage her—much to his brothers' chagrin.

Meadow's voice blared through the intercom. "Uncle Ty, I *love* everything. I really want to learn to paint better. Maybe you could come up here and show me?"

Ty pushed the Talk button. "How about you come down for lunch first? Then I'll give you a lesson."

She scampered into the kitchen just as he set the sandwich plates and bowls of soup on the countertop.

He helped her up onto the stool, pushed her chair closer to the counter and then sat on the stool next to hers. She polished off the meal in minutes, demurely wiped her mouth with the napkin, hopped off the stool and brought her dishes to load in the dishwasher. Ty marveled at how much less work was involved in caring for a seven-year-old than a toddler.

"Ready for my art lesson now?" She trained bright eyes on him.

"Absolutely." He cleared his dishes and then mounted two flights of stairs with Meadow at his side.

Immersing in art on any level brought pleasure and solace to him even during the worst of times. Probably the night before and waking up that morning qualified as worst times. He set a blank canvas on an easel for

173

Meadow and placed a white charcoal pencil in the tray.

"Okay, sweetheart, listen up."

"I'm listening, Uncle Ty. I'm so excited. My teacher said I show a lot of artistic talent."

Echoes of the same compliment he had received as a first grader rang in his mind. "Wow. I'm impressed. Let's see if we can develop that talent."

He picked up the pencil and lightly sketched the tree line viewed through the studio's windows. "One of the methods I use before I paint a scene is sketching like this on the canvas. Then I can add layers of color between the lines. You see how faint the lines are?"

"Uh huh."

"That way you don't see them through the paint. Want to try it?" He handed her the pencil, stepped away from the easel and left her to her drawing.

Ty sat down on the leather chair in the corner of the studio and hung over his cellphone. It was the first time he had checked for messages since leaving the hotel that morning. No word from her. She did say that they could talk when he returned. Well, he had returned. Should he contact her? Wrestling with the pros and cons of a text or phone conversation, he decided to use any means to melt her heart.

He sent her a photo of the new puppy in a text.

—Meet Charlene…Do you think my sister is going to kill me—

Grateful that she responded to him, he hoped that he could fix whatever had gone wrong with her. She had told him that she loved him. Surely there was too much between them to turn their backs on each other. He itched to see her and end the baffling separation between them.

As if the kid had ESP, Meadow provided the perfect

excuse. "Harper said I just *have* to go to the bookstore here. Momma gave me money in my purse to buy books. Can we go, please, Uncle Ty?"

"Well sure. We'll go tomorrow. How does that sound?"

"Good. I want to buy an art book I saw on Amazon."

Cassidy will love that Meadow waited to visit to her store rather than click on the mega-retailer's website.

"It's a deal, princess."

****

His heart skipped a beat when he caught a glimpse of Cassidy behind the counter at her store. He thought the vase of roses on the counter that she had obviously taken with her from the hotel room was a good sign.

"Cozy Nook Books. What a cool name," Meadow said. "It looks so cozy in there."

He held the door open for his niece and her constant companion, Charlene to pass in front of him. Cassidy raised her head and gazed straight into his eyes. What did her somber expression and slightly bloodshot eyes mean? Was she as unhappy as he? Did she long to forget about ruining their romantic weekend? He did.

"Hi, Cassidy," he said.

"Hi," she said softly.

She turned her attention to the little girl. "Hi, Meadow. Welcome to my store. Who do we have here?"

Meadow beamed at Cass. "This is my puppy. Her name is Charlene. She's just like your Charlie only smaller and a girl."

Cass bent to pet the pup's head. "She's a cutey."

"Thank you, Miss Cassidy. Where are the art books? There's one I specially want to buy."

Cass moved from behind the counter. She wore a silky, summer skirt that skimmed mid-calf and a lacy camisole beneath a slightly sheer sleeveless blouse. Lovely. As always. Even though her face wasn't alight with the usual beautiful smile for him. She took Meadow's hand and ushered her to the art section. And then she turned to face him again, doe-eyed, as if she feared what came next.

What comes next?

Slowly she returned to the front of the store taking up a position again behind the counter. A purposeful barrier between them?

He sidled up to the counter and leaned toward her. "I missed you Saturday night. And Sunday morning. I'm still trying to understand why you left."

She cast her eyes downward shaking her head. "I know. I'm so sorry, Ty. I hope you can forgive me."

"I can forgive you anything, Cass. But I need to understand what upset you so much. Can you please explain it to me?"

"Uncle Ty, can I have this one?" Meadow held up a thick book.

"Sure, sweetie. You can have as many books as you want. Go for it."

"Oh boy!"

He shrugged his shoulders. "I guess this isn't the place," Ty said to Cassidy.

"Not ideal."

"Meadow is staying with me for a few days. Will you come to my house this coming weekend for dinner? Please?"

"Yes. I'd like that. Thank you."

The dark cloud that had hung over him lifted. "Good. Great."

Meadow lumbered up to him lugging an armful of books while she clutched Charlene's leash in her hand.

"Whoa. Let me help you." He relieved her of the burden and stacked the books on the counter.

Cassidy scanned each volume and totaled the sale. Meadow dug in her cute little shoulder purse, produced a twenty-dollar bill and held it out to Ty. "Here's the money Momma gave me."

Ty waved the bill away. "You save that, Meadow. I'll treat you today."

"Oh boy. Thank you, Uncle Ty."

"This is really heavy." Cass tested the heft of the plastic bag she had filled with Meadow's bounty.

"I'll carry it." Ty's hand brushed Cass's satiny fingers in the transfer.

An electric zing of attraction passed between them. Cassidy's eyes widened. She felt it, too. Maybe he wouldn't lose her after all.

Appeased that at least she had agreed to see him again, Ty directed his attention down at Meadow. "Ready to go paint some more, sweetie?"

"Yep."

"Okay. Thank you, Cass. See you soon."

"Thank you, Miss Cassidy."

"Bye Meadow." She smiled at his niece. The light for a few brief moments returned to her jade eyes. "Bye, Ty."

It was hard for him to turn his back on Cassidy but there was nothing left to say until they were alone. He opened the passenger door of his truck for Meadow and then stowed her books in the back seat.

Ty had just started the engine when Meadow said, "Did you see the man in the store? There was a man sitting at the table in the corner kind of staring at you when you talked with Miss Cassidy."

Chapter 20

Ty faced Meadow. "You saw a man in the bookstore?"

How did I miss that?

"Yes. I saw him in the back by the books when we first came in and then I saw him in the front of the store sitting at the table when you were talking to Miss Cassidy. He looked kind of mean. Didn't you see him?"

"No. I didn't see anyone." He turned off the truck engine. His mind raced needing to get to Cassidy and make sure all was well.

"We forgot to give Miss Cassidy the toy that we bought for Charlie at PetSmart. I'll run it in to her real quick. Are you okay to stay here by yourself for a couple minutes?"

"Sure. Can I look at some of my new books?"

"Of course."

He reached into the back seat and hoisted the bag of books up from the floor behind Meadow's seat. He placed the bag at her feet. "Here you go. I'll be right back."

Ty opened the driver's door after he cracked open his window a couple inches and slipped out of his seat. He grabbed the first dog toy out of the shopping bag in the rear compartment that his hand touched and then he hurried to the bookstore. His heart thundered so hard in his chest that he thought he might crack a rib.

His stomach sank when he didn't see Cassidy through the glass behind the front counter where he had left her just a few minutes before. Concern mounted when she didn't appear as the bell on the front door jingled opening it. He stepped inside the shop and closed the door behind him.

"Cass!" he called out. "Cassie, it's Ty!"

He heard no clear answer, but he thought he caught a faint sound coming from somewhere in the back of the store. Ty tossed the dog toy onto the counter by the register and continued the search heading toward her office and the storage room. He called out her name again.

A noise came from behind the closed door of the storage room. He pounded on the door and then tested turning the knob. The door opened just a crack meeting some kind of resistance.

"Cassidy are you in there?"

"Yes," came her muffled response.

He put his shoulder against the door and pushed harder. It budged a couple more inches.

"Are you okay? What happened?" Ty continued to shove at the door.

"I'm fine. One of the storage shelves split and gave way. It's lodged behind the door. Let me keep moving some cartons aside and then I can drag it free."

"I'll help you. Give me a minute. I'll be right back."

He rushed out to his truck, grabbed his tool box out of the trunk, closed the hatch and hustled to the passenger door.

Ty opened the door and leaned inside. "Miss Cassidy has a problem in her store, and I have to help her," he told Meadow. "I don't want to leave you and

Charlene alone in the car, so come back with me, okay?"

"Okay. I still have Mommy's money, so maybe I will find another book."

She gave him an impish grin. "Or two."

Ty chuckled and ruffled her white blonde hair, so like his sister's. He ushered his niece and her energetic puppy back inside Cozy Nook leaving Meadow to wander among the bookshelves while he returned to Cassidy. She had managed to open the door enough for him to squeeze through into the storage area where he found her bent over, dragging boxes and then stacking them in the corner of the room.

Her hair had come loose from the bun on the top of her head, her long, silk skirt was ripped at the bottom and a trickle of blood ran down her leg. She paused in her work and looked up at him, her face flushed with exertion. Even bedraggled, she looked downright beautiful. Ty drew her into his arms and hugged her tightly.

"You're bleeding," he said.

"I know. Caught my skirt and leg on a jagged edge of the shelf." She nestled her head on his chest, a perfect fit.

"I'm so happy you came back." She arched her neck and looked up at him. "Why did you?"

"Meadow told me that she saw a strange man in a couple of places in the store when we were talking. I didn't notice anyone else here. She described him as mean looking. I thought maybe you were in trouble."

`The color instantly drained from her face. "Oh no, perfectly safe here," she stammered.

"There were several folks in the shop browsing around today. Didn't buy a thing. I'm sure Meadow saw one of them. Where *is* Meadow by the way? Did she bring the puppy back, too?" she rattled off.

"That kid goes nowhere without Charlene. She's looking for more books. According to her proclamation, 'Uncle Ty you can never have too many books.'"

"That's a girl after my own heart. I need lots more customers like her."

Her sunny smile lit her face, and the color returned to her cheeks. *Irresistible.*

Ty couldn't resist. He dipped his head and kissed her losing himself for a few brief moments in her sweetness.

But she had a cut on her leg that needed tending and a clean-up job that needed finishing—not to mention a child who could appear at any moment and turn privacy into PDA.

He forced himself to let her go and then started to drag and stack boxes away from the felled shelf. Cassidy bent over a box to pitch in, but Ty stopped her. He set one of the kindergarten chairs that she used at the kids' story hours on the floor in front of her.

"You sit. I'll have this done in a few minutes. Then we'll fix your leg."

Ty made quick work of clearing the area blocking the door so that it swung fully open. "You're going to need to have the wall patched and plastered before you can put up a new shelf. I can do it for you if you want."

"I don't think I want another shelf hung there. I'll think about what I want to do with this room another time. Thank you, Ty. I would have been stuck here much longer if you hadn't showed up."

"Miss Cassidy, are you okay?" Meadow stood in the doorway.

"Yes, I am, thank you. And most of all thank you for

coming back to rescue me." Cassidy rose from the chair.

Her leg wobbled slightly spurring Ty to shoot out his arm to steady her. "Let's take a look at that cut. Do you have a first aid kit?"

"I do. On a shelf under the register."

"I'll get it." Meadow ran ahead of them holding her puppy's leash in her hand. Charlene skittered behind her mistress clamping the toy Ty had brought into the store for Charlie in her mouth. The squeaky octopus was just about as big as she was.

Ty wrapped an arm around Cassidy's shoulder and led her to the front of the store into the alcove.

She leaned lightly against his side. "There's no need to fuss. I'm fine."

"I'll be the judge of that."

"Yes, Doctor." Cass sat down at the table.

"I'll play doctor with you anytime." He winked, amused at her embarrassed blush.

Meadow bustled over to the alcove and handed Ty the first aid kit. He kneeled in front of Cassidy and folded the hem of her skirt up over her knee. Using an antiseptic wipe to clean the blood away, he examined the long, jagged scrape on her lower calf.

If Meadow weren't hanging over his shoulder, he might have stroked the satiny skin on Cassie's leg...up...up. He tamped down the temptation with the little girl hovering.

"Oh, look Uncle Ty. There are Hello Kitty band aids in here." She displayed a handful that she took out of the kit.

"I think we need one big bandage on this." Ty reached for a package of gauze.

Meadow pouted.

"I love your idea," Cass said. "I'll bet the Hello Kitty band aids will make me feel better right away. I think we should use them, Ty. Thank you for the suggestion, Meadow."

The kid's frown turned upside down.

Ty forced himself to exhibit Herculean patience covering the length of the cut with multiple kids' band aids. "Nurse" Meadow laboriously opened each one of many and handed them to him like his right hand in the OR. Good thing the cut was superficial, or Cassidy would have bled out long ago while the bandaging dragged on.

"Now you have to kiss it," Meadow commanded. "Mommy always does to make it feel all better. It works."

Ty sat back on his heels and arched his eyebrows at Cass. "I'll bet I can think of lots of ways to make it feel all better."

Meadow folded her arms and stood ramrod straight next to Ty, a little drill sergeant unwilling to budge until he delivered the feel better kiss.

He took gentle hold of the back of Cassidy's calf, bent his head and planted the lightest kiss on one Hello Kitty.

"You know what my mom always did to make me feel better?" Cassidy draped her skirt over the injury, her cheeks flaming red from his eyebrow arching innuendo.

She narrowed her eyes at Ty forestalling any more suggestive comments.

"What?" Meadow said.

"My mom always let me eat as many cookies as I wanted." She got up from the chair, paced behind the front counter and brought out a tin from under the register.

"I'm sorry, Meadow. I don't have any of your Nana's cookies left, but I do have my favorite." She popped off the top of the tin.

Meadow clapped her hands. "Oreos are my favorite. too. Don't tell Nana."

"Help yourself." Cassidy stuffed a whole, double-stuffed cookie into her mouth.

Ty's eyes widened watching her and then he burst out laughing. "Now that's impressive. Are you trying to kill me?"

Cassidy covered her mouth and barked out a laugh. "Oh my gosh, I spit cookie all over my hand."

"Does your cut feel better?" Meadow said.

"It hardly hurts at all. Your uncle's kiss must be magic." Cassidy smiled.

"If my Nana was here, she could make your leg back to normal right away. One day when I was at her house I fell in the backyard and scraped my knee. Nana put a band aid on it. Then she put her hand over the band aid and like magic it didn't hurt at all any more. And then she kissed it just to make sure the hurt didn't come back."

Ty keyed in on Meadow's chatter. He'd have to leave fast before she divulged any more magical family secrets. "Did you find any more books to buy, Meadow?"

'No. I think I have all I want for now."

"Then let's go to my house and fix Charlene something to eat. I don't think my laces are good for her." Charlene lay across Ty's feet energetically chewing on the laces in his sneakers.

Meadow giggled, scooped Charlene up into her arms and snuggled the wiggling puppy.

Cassidy gave Meadow a hug. "Thank you for helping me with my cut. It hardly hurts at all."

"Thank you for the cookies. Maybe you can bring Charlie to Uncle Ty's next barbecue, and he can meet Charlene."

"I would love to. I bet Charlie will love Charlene. I already know he loves anything your uncle cooks on the grill."

"I can't wait to see Charlie again. Bye, Miss Cassidy." The little girl smiled and headed for the door.

"Thanks so much for helping me, Ty."

"Always. We're still on for dinner Saturday, right?"

"Yes. Can I bring anything?"

"Only your beautiful self." He smiled, bussed her cheek, grabbed his tool box which he hadn't even opened and walked away with Meadow in tow.

****

Cassidy stood in the bookstore window and looked out at Ty driving by honking and waving. She touched the spot on her cheek dreamily where his lips had rested. Despite her roller coaster emotions for days after the showing, a simple touch or steamy kiss from Ty had her yearning for more.

She hadn't told him how hard she had landed on the floor under the shelf, not wanting to make a bigger deal of her predicament. But her body hurt all over. Maybe a couple of Advil would help to relieve the ache in her back. She moved at a sluggish pace to her office and took the bottle of pills out of her desk drawer. Cass washed down two tablets with a swig of cold coffee.

The phone rang. She smiled at the caller ID.

"Hi, Joelle."

"Hi, Cass, how are you today?"

"I'm doing great."

Cassidy told her about Ty and Meadow's visit and how she had taken her advice and was having dinner with Ty.

"I thought you were going to the Cubs game. Isn't that tonight?" Cass said.

"Yes. I'm calling from the car."

"Thanks for checking in. Have the best time. Go Cubs!"

"Go Cubs!"

Cassidy went back into the storage room, steering clear of the remaining shelving just in case, to look through the boxes for the notecards and bookmarks shipment. She had plenty of room to display them on the new bookcase Mickey had made for her.

She carried two small boxes out to the front of the store. When she got there, she gasped and dropped the boxes on the floor. Sawyer leaned against the counter. He looked fit and sexy in a pair of tight black jeans, black boots and a black T-shirt that molded to the defined muscles of his chest. A lazy smile crinkled the corners of his eyes.

Maybe I hit my head harder than I thought.

"You aren't hallucinating, love," he said.

He looked so solid, so *alive*. Meadow had seen him, too. *Did that make this more or less impossible?*

Tears tracked her cheeks, and she had a hard time catching her breath. "Why are you here, Sawyer?"

"Because you still need me."

"I'll always need you."

He remained silent.

"I will always love you," Cassidy whispered.

"And I will always…" His voice lowered and he

said faintly, "love you."

"Please don't leave me." She sensed he was about to. But she needed to understand—wanted to rush into his arms.

Was he really with her in body and spirit. *What is this?*

"I won't leave you until it's time." His voice was so soft that she could barely hear it.

"How will I know it is time?" Cass took a step closer to him.

But in an instant he was suddenly…just gone.

Chapter 21

Meadow had seen Sawyer. Cass was still astounded. She had believed that she had imagined him into her world as a private fantasy from the depths of her grief. She wanted Sawyer to stay with her beyond his death, and her imagination had made that possible. He wasn't really real.

But now?... Was he *really* "living" at the bookstore? Would other customers see him? Recognize him? Never in her wildest dreams would she have believed that Cozy Nook Books might wind up a stop on a ghost tour.

Cassidy had looked forward to the dinner at Ty's house all week with equal portions of anticipation and dread. The evening could end with reconciliation, or she might tell Ty goodbye. Since he had left the bookstore after Meadow's encounter with Sawyer, she had tried but hadn't succeeded to grasp Sawyer's haunting her and Ty's unwitting place in the spectral love triangle.

Did Sawyer want to eternally keep Cassidy for himself? His appearances at the store gave her peace and banished her grief and made her feel loved. But Ty owned her heart as much as Sawyer. Would she ever feel free to give her whole heart to Ty while Sawyer still fleetingly lingered in her life? And what about Ty's artistic connection to Sawyer? How could he have duplicated an image that he couldn't possibly have ever seen?

She had dressed for an evening out on the town choosing to wear a breezy summer midi-dress and high-heeled sandals, rather than shorts and running shoes for a likely casual dinner in his home. But Cass wanted to look her best. Maybe to buoy her confidence. Maybe to just feel special with the special man. Even if it was for the last time.

Cass opened her marriage memento drawer, extracted Sawyer's wallet and dropped it in her purse wanting proof of Ty's plagiarism and invasion of her privacy. How he'd explain himself, she had no clue.

Walking the lake path in heels didn't appeal to Cass. She drove the circuit to his house in a few minutes, rang his bell and stood on Ty's doorstep, a bundle of nerves and confusion. When he swung open his door and stood in front of her, all thoughts of Sawyer or any other man evaporated. Ty. Only Ty.

He didn't wear shorts and running shoes, either, but rather pressed slacks, a pin-striped dress shirt tucked into a belted waist with the sleeves rolled up so that his muscular forearms dusted with sable hair were exposed—*very* sexy to Cass.

"You look so beautiful. Please. Come in," he said.

Instead of stepping aside for her to pass in front of him, he reached out, gently clasped her hand and drew her toward him.

She stepped into his foyer allowing him to lead her on a path straight into his arms. He tightened his embrace and kicked the door shut with his foot. Cass hugged Ty back, melting in the compelling rush of connection with him. Her body molded to his, a perfect fit with her head nestled in the crook of his shoulder and her breasts flattened against the hard planes of his chest. He rested his chin on her crown and just held her while neither of them uttered a sound and the clock ticked away seconds.

Cassidy didn't like confrontations, and she skirted them whenever possible. In his arms, the last thing she wanted to do was broach the subject of the boudoir painting. But she had to explain why she had abandoned him at the showing, and he *had* to explain what caused her to leave. She loosened her hold on him. He read the cue and released the hug.

But he didn't disconnect from her entirely. Ty wrapped an arm around her shoulders and paced with her to the back of the house. He had set the kitchen table for two facing each other with placemats, utensils, napkins and glassware. A three-wick candle flickered at the center of the table infusing the air with a light vanilla scent. The summer days were shortening, but there was still enough light remaining in the dusky shadows for a view of the tree-rimmed lake beyond his sliding glass doors. A perfect scene.

Except for the pressing questions weighing on both their minds the past week that hung over them like a presence in the room.

She sat in the chair that he pulled out for her plopping her purse onto the chair next to her. Cass had no appetite, but she eagerly took a sip of the red wine that breathed in a goblet at her place setting.

Ty produced two dinner plates from his refrigerator brimming with salad greens and topped with strips of grilled chicken. He set the food down on the placemats and then took his seat across from her. Lifting his wineglass, he proposed a simple, "Cheers."

Cass clinked his glass with hers, repeated the toast and took another fortifying sip. Ty held up a basket of bread offering her a slice of sour dough. She didn't want it, but she accepted a piece and set it down on the edge of her dinner plate.

The gap between them needed bridging and Cassidy had struck out that evening intending to eliminate the strange love triangle that she was caught up in one way or another—choose to continue living in her memories with Sawyer or turn her back on the past and commit to the unknown with Ty. The choice would be far easier if Sawyer's spirit didn't interfere.

Her heart wouldn't cooperate in the decision. In Ty's company all she wanted was the present and the future with him. When Sawyer materialized, her bottomless love for him rekindled and she longed to stay with him forever.

She knew Ty wanted an explanation of her behavior the night of the showing. But instead of grilling her, he kept the conversation light.

"Meadow is in love with your store." He chuckled. "She's in love with you, too, for that matter."

"Aw. She's a cutie. I love when kids have a passion for reading. Kindred souls."

"She's a passionate kid. I really enjoyed being with her this week. But I missed you…" He trailed off reaching across the table to clasp her hands.

The connection to him had the usual swirling, comforting, core-tugging effect on Cass. And he had missed her. The feeling was painfully mutual.

Cassidy picked up her purse and put it in her lap. "Ty. I want to explain why I left you on Saturday night." She gazed steadily into his blue-gray eyes.

He wagged his head, his eyes soft. "I've thought about it a lot since Saturday night. You don't need to explain, Cass. I figured since Sawyer showed his work at LM Galleries, too, my event dredged up painful emotions for you. I don't blame you for wanting to escape that."

"No…it was…"

"I only wish I were more available to you that night. I could've helped you handle whatever you were going through," he interjected. "One minute you were browsing the showing and the next I couldn't find you."

"I know…"

"Hang on. That reminds me. I have something for you." Ty withdrew the handhold and shoved his chair away from the table.

With a few powerful strides he disappeared from view into the front of the house. He returned moments later carrying a wrapped canvas which he presented to her.

"Oh, Ty. The cardinals painting I loved." Cass rose from her seat setting her purse aside, placed the canvas on the table to the left of her place setting and began tearing off the wrapping paper.

"Nope. But I hope you like it," he said.

She finished unwrapping and revealed the painting of her on her honeymoon. She closed her eyes and took a deep, shaky breath.

When she opened them Ty stared at her, questions swimming in his eyes. "You *don't* like it, I see."

"No, no. It's lovely. It's only…"

"The woman there reminds me of you. I thought maybe you'd see the resemblance, too."

Cass sat back down on her chair facing him. "She *is* me, Ty. This painting is the reason why I left on Saturday."

"What do you mean?"

She took Sawyer's wallet out of her purse, opened the bifold, dug her fingers behind the credit card slots and slipped out the photo of the painting while Ty watched her every move. Cass handed it to him without a word.

Ty knit his brows, bent his head over the picture and studied it, his gaze flicking between the painting and the photograph a few times.

He handed the photo back to her. "Sawyer's?"

"Yes. Taken of me in our hotel room the first morning of our honeymoon. The Eiffel Tower is visible out that window."

"I see."

"That's all you have to say? How in the world did you steal this *very* private image?"

"Steal?" Ty crossed his arms and leaned back in his chair. "I didn't. Trust me, Cass. I've never seen that photograph until this minute."

Frustrated and incredulous she blurted out, "How can I believe that? The painting is *exactly* the same. Sawyer developed that photo in his darkroom and made only that copy, which he kept in his wallet. I never took it out after he died. Until I came home Saturday night after I saw your copy hanging on the gallery wall. I couldn't fathom how you could invade my privacy so completely. I still can't."

"Ah, now I understand."

"Well enlighten me. I don't understand at all."

"Let me tell you about my family…"

"Seriously, Ty? What do those sweet people have to do with this?"

"Not directly." He leaned toward her and clasped

both her hands again. "Bear with me. Okay?"

She slowly nodded agreement, prepared to doubt every word.

"This was the first painting I created in my new studio upstairs. Day one after moving in. That was a little over a year ago. The image—your image—just appeared in my head fully formed. I hadn't met you. I hadn't seen you around town. When I finished the painting, I decided it was just for me. After I met you, it had even more meaning to me because the woman reminded me of you. I guess I received a vision of the woman I was destined to meet…and fall in love with.

"The courier picked up that painting by mistake. I never meant to show it. Anywhere. I love you Cassidy. I would never do anything to hurt or embarrass you."

She widened her eyes. *This doesn't make sense.*

He read her mind. "I know this sounds crazy. But in my family it makes perfect sense."

"Really? I don't see how."

Ty wove a tale about identical female triplets in the Binder family, his family, inheriting fantastical powers dating back to the Golden Age of Piracy in the early 18th century. These *Sisters of the Legend* as babies could morph into butterflies and pygmy ponies. Cousins could communicate with sea creatures and turn into marine animals. The entire family had rampant creative talents. His mom and aunt had uncanny extrasensory perception.

"Maybe some of my mother's precognition has rubbed off on me. That explains my receiving a prophetic vision of you that I produced on that canvas," he concluded.

If Cass hadn't experienced visions of Sawyer, her own fantastical tale, she would have grabbed her purse and run for the door. But every word that Ty had just said rang true for her.

Tension evaporated as she accepted his explanation. "Thank you, Ty. I understand completely now."

"You do?"

"Yes. And I'm sorry for making such a big deal about this. The painting is beautiful."

"Is it okay if I come over there and ravish you? I want you in my arms."

She huffed a delighted laugh. "Hold that thought. I have some explaining to do, too."

"Yeah? I'm listening."

"You know how I told you the story of how Sawyer and I first met?"

"The book signing. Yes. We have that in common."

"True. You both also signed books in the same location in the store, the alcove."

"Okay."

"Well. It's not every minute or even every day, but it seems that Sawyer lives there. At Cozy Nook Books."

"Meadow…"

"Right. Meadow saw him the other day. And after you both left, I did, too. He spoke to me, Ty."

"So…what does this mean to you, Cass? To us?"

"I do love you, Ty…"

"Why do I have the feeling that there's a 'but' in there?"

Her conflicting emotions swamped her. She wanted to divide her heart in two and give one whole piece to Ty and the other to Sawyer.

Chapter 22

She gave him a tremulous smile. Ty's pulse raced at what she'd say next. He had no problem competing with flesh and blood men like fix-up date, Jack. But the heaven-perfected spirit of her loving husband? Nothing in Ty's realm of experience prepared him for that contest. Still. Winning Cassidy's heart—exclusively—was worth it to him.

"I don't know why Sawyer is still in my life, Ty. But he is. And while he is, it's not fair to expect you to…" She frowned, apparently at a loss to finish the sentence.

"What? Share you with him?"

Cass pursed her lips and nodded, yes.

"I don't want to share you with anyone. I'm coming over there."

He couldn't leave his seat and skirt the table fast enough. When he reached her, she arched her neck and gazed up at him, her shoulders hunched. Her vulnerable demeanor was heartbreaking. Tears shimmered in her rounded lawn green eyes. She looked so soft, so pretty, so breakable.

During one short summer Cassidy had become the center of Ty's world. He hadn't spent a single day or night since they had met without her monopolizing his thoughts and dreams and he had even toyed with the idea of proposing to her during their weekend in Chicago. Ty had scoped out possible engagement rings online at

Tiffany and Cartier on Michigan Avenue thinking that she might have agreed to pick one out before returning to Redbird.

He understood that no one, himself included, could ever replace Sawyer in her heart. But maybe she might reserve a place in her heart only for him and give new love a chance. There was no way he'd let her go without a fight.

Ty grasped the rungs of the ladder-back chair where she sat and turned her sideways to the table. Then he knelt down at her eye level and took both of her hands in his. He gazed deeply into her eyes hoping that she could read the depth of his feelings just by meeting his gaze.

"Cass, do you love me enough to hear me out? Can you give me a chance to convince you that we can work things out?"

"I…" More tears welled in her eyes. But she nodded, yes.

"I will never compete with Sawyer's memory or prevent you from honoring his memory however you choose. Your marriage and life with him are yours alone. I haven't had that kind of love in my life. Until I met you. So now I understand what he meant to you—and you to him.

"I told Kane shortly after the book signing that you were special—uniquely special. The one for me. I didn't have a single doubt that I had fallen in love with you from the first. And to my surprise I kept falling in love with you more and more. I suspect I'll love you more tomorrow and then the next day…I want forever with you, Cass."

She slipped her hands away and covered her face. Her shoulders shook as she sobbed softly. It killed him to make her cry. Especially since he wasn't sure what her crying meant. Was it ripping her apart to tell him thanks but no thanks? Or possibly were they tears of joy?

Cass finally raised her head and regarded him. He thumbed tears away from the corners of her eyes waiting for some response.

"I don't know what to say. Is this a…proposal?"

"If you want it to be."

"I don't know what I want, Ty. Except to be fair to you. How can you possibly accept all the weirdness that I told you about?"

"Can you accept my weirdness?"

"Well…sure. But where does that leave us?"

He flexed his legs and stood up. Ty stepped over to the kitchen counter to pluck a tissue out of the box that he kept there.

She accepted the tissue that he handed her, swiped it under each eye and then blew her nose daintily. Cass gazed up at him.

"Do you want to finish dinner?" he said.

Cass crinkled her nose. "Not particularly."

"Let me put these plates back in the fridge for later and then we can leave."

"Where are we going?"

"I want to meet Sawyer."

"Ty, my god. I don't know…"

"Trust me, Cass. I won't say anything to hurt him or you. But for me, this has to happen. Okay?" He held out his hand to her, mightily pleased when she placed her tiny hand in his and stood up.

****

Neither spoke during the brief trip to Cozy Nook Books. Ty could feel Cassidy's nervous energy thrumming from her seat next to him. The gas light replicas that lined Park Avenue provided enough light at the front of her shop for her to unlock the door.

They walked into the gloomy interior of the store—a perfect environment for a real-life ghost story. Cass fired up the soft lighting in the alcove highlighting that the place was empty. Ty may have grown up in an extraordinary paranormal family, but that didn't prepare him to conjure a spirit from another realm.

He turned to Cassidy. "How do you make him come to you?"

She shrugged her shoulders and then crossed her arms over her chest as if she were cold. "I don't. It just happens sometimes."

Ty was on his own. He wasn't afraid of Sawyer's ghost, but maybe his bravery was misplaced. *Could he punch me in the nose?*

Only one way to find out.

"Sawyer," he said, his tone conversational. "You may have seen me here with Cass the past few months. May I talk with you now?"

Nothing happened, at least that Ty detected. Maybe only Cassidy and little kids could see the guy.

"Is he here, Cass?"

"Uh uh."

"What should I do?"

"I'm not…" She clamped her mouth shut.

The blurry silhouette of a man materialized about five feet in front of Ty. And then the blurriness clarified into sharp focus. Sawyer Finnegan stared at Ty wearing an unreadable expression on his face.

Ty kept his body loose and gazed back at him, hopefully conveying non-threatening amiability. "I wanted to meet you. I'm glad I have."

"Why?" Sawyer's voice was every bit as clear and strong as Ty's. Just two alpha males meeting nose to nose.

He respected Sawyer for all the man had accomplished in life artistically and for having loved the same woman that Ty loved deeply. They had a lot in common, but he doubted that fact would interest Sawyer. Clearly Ty invaded romantic territory.

Would she stand with him to face her former husband? Ty held out his hand to Cassidy and gazed deeply into her eyes hoping she'd accept a handhold and present a united front to Sawyer. She didn't disappoint him.

With her hand firmly clasped in his, Ty faced Sawyer again. "I'm in love with Cassidy, Sawyer. And I want to make a life with her."

Sawyer shifted his attention to Cassidy. Gazing at her, his features transformed. Unmistakable adoration shone in the man's eyes. Their history together flowed between them like a tender current.

"Do you love him?" Sawyer said.

Cassidy gripped Ty's hand tighter. His heart was in his mouth awaiting her reply.

"Yes, I do." Her voice trembled but she remained dry-eyed. "I want to make a life with him, too."

A smile spread widely on Sawyer's lips, a beautiful, heart-breaking gift to her and Ty. "Then, now it's time."

Sawyer disappeared.

For a couple of breathless moments Ty and Cassidy just stood there holding each other's hands.

And then she faced him. Cass's eyes held a sheen of tears, but she smiled at him radiantly, threw her arms around his neck, and buried her head against his chest. He pressed her to his heart sending up a prayer of thanksgiving to the heavens where Sawyer probably dwelled.

She raised her head, gazed up at him through damp eyelashes and grinned, her eyes dancing. "You were saying when you were down on your knees in your kitchen?"

Thank you for purchasing
this publication of The Wild Rose Press, Inc.

For questions or more information
contact us at
info@thewildrosepress.com.

The Wild Rose Press, Inc.
www.thewildrosepress.com